The Last Months
of
Violet Koski

Heather Smith

BookReality
Helping Writers Become Independent Authors

For Linda

Gabriel and the Fairy Ring

Mallorca and Ireland 1983

It was Thursday, the day Gabriel went to his grandmother's for lunch. Her house was just around the corner from the primary school, so he didn't need to be picked up by his mother, who was usually blowing with impatience at his lingering back in the playground. She would grab him brusquely by the arm and say:

'How come you're always the last one out?'

His grandmother Cliona never asked the kind of question he couldn't answer. And she didn't ask how he got on at school either.

He ambled along the pavements of the housing estate, counting the weeds that sprouted from the cracks and making sure not to tread on any deadly processionary caterpillars. It was March, and there was a fine layer of yellow dust on the path and on the swings in the children's playground to his right. He stopped beside a parked car and wrote his name on the rear window, and then inspected the pollen stain on his forefinger. In March his Irish grandmother never failed to complain about 'the number of fecking pine trees on this goddamn island.'

When Gabriel reached the house, he looked to see if her car was parked outside. Every week he checked the Dublin plaque on the rear window and the mess of odd sweaters, wicker baskets and English textbooks on the back seat. And there it was, a dusty old Renault parked in front of the flat-roofed house where the tiles were glinting orange in the afternoon sun. Once assured all was in order, he ran his fingers over the flaking green paint of the front gate and pushed it open. He liked the feel of the cold metal and how it screeched on the rusty hinges, and he liked the solidity of the rough-cut stone columns that supported the porch where Cliona now stood, sneezing and swearing.

'Well, there you are, my child. Come and give me a hug. Lunch is ready and we'll eat as soon as I can stop sneezing!'

Gabriel dropped his bag and observed her streaming eyes and red nose.

'And just what are you waiting for? It's my allergy. Don't you know by now?'

He embraced her comforting belly and asked what was for lunch.

She laughed. 'The same as you've been having for the last three years every Thursday.'

It was spaghetti with tomato sauce and grated cheese: his favourite, but frowned upon by his mother, a nervous health fiend who feared all non-ecological, white, refined products like they were Lucifer himself. So Thursday at Cliona's was the Eden of all forbidden foods; gorge yourself without one second of remorse.

While Cliona cleared the long kitchen table of English textbooks, notebooks, pens and everything else that pointed to her recent class, Gabriel went into the living room and looked at the picture on the wall. This was the final part of the ritual: the five-minute observation of an enlarged, framed photo which hung over the fireplace. Since he could remember, Gabriel had associated his grandmother's house with this luminous picture of a fairy ring, which gradually became so magically alive to him that it was the only real thing in the room, even more so than himself. He imagined standing in front of the hawthorn tree in the first light of the morning, a fresh breeze gently moving its white flowers; and he could touch, in awe, the stones that formed a circle around the tree, the undeniable proof that here was a fairy ring where the Little People entered their underground dwelling. For Gabriel had no doubt that they existed.

'Lunch is on the table, Gabriel!'

Cliona observed her only grandson. He was a quiet, delicate-looking child, small for his age and prone to daydreaming. On the days when he was especially silent he would stand in front of the photo for longer and seem to gather comfort from it. Today was one of those days. She didn't hurry him, and let him have his fill. Cliona remembered that the photo was one of the first objects that had entered the house thirty-five years back, when she had left Ireland and married a Mallorcan. It was the first thing that everyone looked at when they went into her airy living room. And she noted with a certain smug pleasure how the image of the wilds of Ireland had slowly permeated the whitewashed walls so that its counterparts, amateur paintings of Mallorcan seascapes, were not even given a cursory glance. The scene at Lough Brin, in County Kerry, had been captured at dawn by a renowned Irish photographer; low mists retreating to the mountains so that the first light rested without hindrance on a blooming hawthorn tree, around which was a circle of greyish white boulders. No visitor escaped the spell of that photograph.

'Would you like me to tell you the story of fairy rings again?' She piled his plate with spaghetti.

Gabriel nodded and began to devour the steaming pasta and melting cheese.

'When you're out for a walk in the Irish countryside, you must always keep your eyes wide open and be sure not to step inside a fairy ring. They are gateways to the land of the fairies, and it is said that underground there are fairy cities. Sometimes you'll see a wide circle of big toadstools; other times it'll be a circle of stones, like the one in my photo. But there must always be a hawthorn tree in the middle; otherwise it's not a true fairy ring.'

'And what would happen if you stepped inside accidentally?' asked Gabriel.

'Ah, well, that is a difficult question to answer. Inside the ring the fairies gather to sing and dance, have feasts and have their meetings. People who can hear them say they sing all night with high, silvery voices. But they don't like being disturbed by humans. If we do, they might play tricks on us, and then they split their sides laughing, for they have a wicked sense of humour and just love to be wild and free.'

Gabriel lifted his head from the plate. His black eyes stared at her from his small white face.

'You mean they make fun of people, like the kids at school do? Are they nasty, then?'

'No, no, they're not like us humans, little one. But nobody knows for sure. There are stories that tell of people who disappeared when they stepped inside the ring. They were never seen again.'

'Maybe they went to a magic place that's much nicer than here. That's why they didn't come back. Can you talk to the fairies from outside the ring?'

'Gabriel, you have to have special powers to be able to see the fairies and talk to them. I don't know of anyone, to be sure! But I've heard that they may show themselves if you are good to animals and if you care for the earth. And they are especially fond of children who have pure hearts.'

'Why are there no fairy rings in Mallorca?' solemn-eyed Gabriel asked.

'I can't give you an exact answer there, but I think the fairies don't like mosquitoes or the heat,' she said, heaping more spaghetti onto his plate.

'Remember you said you'd take me to Ireland this summer? For my birthday, will you take me to a fairy ring, Granny? Like the one in the photo? That will be my present. Just you and me, okay?'

'Of course I remember! I'll do my best to take you to the one in Kerry, and you'll get another present. Now, finish your lunch. We both need a siesta before your mam comes to collect you.' She rapidly began to clear away the evidence of their meal.

Later that evening, when Gabriel had gone home, Cliona had an inclination to watch an old Disney favourite, *Darby O' Gill and the Little People*. She was just sinking into the sofa in front of the television when the phone rang. It was her daughter, Rosa. She does it on purpose, thought Cliona as she braced herself for the tirade.

'Mum, for Christ's sake, will you stop putting all those stupid ideas about fairy rings into Gabriel's head. Things are bad enough at school already. The teacher says he's locked in his own little world and the other kids think he's a weirdo. If he starts going on about fairy rings, they'll make fun of him. Why can't I have a normal child?'

'Holy Mother of God, Rosa, he's nine years old. Why shouldn't he be fascinated by fairy rings? And have you ever asked yourself why he doesn't interact with the other kids? The little sods are more than likely bullying him.'

'Well, the teacher has said nothing about bullying. She says he ought to visit the school psychologist. And you're just making it worse by pandering to all his fantasies. If Dad were alive, he'd soon put a stop to all this bloody nonsense.'

'And do you think the teacher has noticed if he's being bullied or not? They won't do it in front of her, will they? If the poor child wants to believe in fairies, then let him. I did at his age and it did me no harm. He's just very sensitive and needs special attention. If you weren't always so stressed and had more time for him, you might find out what's wrong.'

'Oh, I can hardly get a word out of him and neither can his father. You're the one he communicates with most, but I'm beginning to think you're a bad influence. And if you have to give him pasta, make sure it's made from wholewheat. The processed stuff you give him just makes him nervous.'

'You can bet it's not my pasta that's making him nervous,' said Cliona and slammed the phone down.

I'm taking Gabriel with me to Kerry this summer, she thought, and we're finding that fairy ring in Lough Brin if it's the last thing I do. She turned off the TV and pondered. How would she get to that area from Dublin, where her brother lived, and how would she find the fairy ring? It wouldn't be easy to find the exact spot. Maybe her brother would help her, but it was just her and Gabriel who would make the trip. She knew this was like a pilgrimage for the child, and she would make sure no one contaminated it with the slurries of their practical, unimaginative minds.

She closed the faded green shutters and went up the stone stairway to bed. March nights were still cold and soon she was under her patchwork quilt. It was good having the double bed to herself and she felt no guilt about not missing her husband. And she had the freedom to take her only grandson to Ireland without him controlling their every move.

Thursdays came and went, pasta was devoured and Gabriel's mother continued to complain. But nothing turned a hair on Cliona's greying red mane, nor did her round countenance lose its half-smile. She noticed how Gabriel developed a look of contentment and imagined he was feeding on the joy of their secret trip, memorising the smallest details as he stood in front of the photo of the fairy ring.

And then, quite unexpectedly, he began to draw. What he drew most were stones and trees. First, he sketched the old olive tree in Cliona's garden. He liked the flaky texture of the bark and the narrow silver-coloured leaves; how the ripe black olives dropped from the branches overhanging the pavement outside the house and were crushed by passers-by, and how his grandmother would constantly grumble as she swept them up. He liked to assemble odd-shaped stones in the garden and draw their sharp edges or polished roundness. Before he sketched, he would hold them and let his palm caress their essence. They all throbbed differently, he thought, and he marvelled that even stones have hearts. When he had finished drawing, he placed them in a circle around the olive tree and watched how the sun weaved its way through the quivering leaves and speckled the stones with pale gold.

Cliona would observe him discreetly from the kitchen. She knew best to make no comments in case he shied away like a nervous sparrow. She was surprised by the accurate delicacy of his drawings and decided she would encourage him. There's no doubting the child's got talent there, she thought, and wondered why nobody had noticed at his progressive, private school. It was one of the first trilingual schools that taught in English, Spanish and Mallorcan, and supposedly developed the budding talents of its pupils. Gabriel's parents struggled to pay the extortionate fees for an education which, in Cliona's shrewd eyes, seemed to be making her grandchild more withdrawn and less sociable.

'Look what I've bought you,' she said one Thursday in May after a large plateful of pale spaghetti stained with blood-red tomato sauce.

She placed on the table a flat oblong package with a hump in the middle.

Gabriel looked dismayed.

'But it's not my birthday yet and you know I want to go to the fairy ring in Kerry for my present! You promised.'

'And what makes you think it's a birthday present? Just open it, will you?'

Gabriel slowly removed the brown paper. It was a professional sketch pad with a black and red hard cover. The hump was a small case with six fine sketching pencils inside, all sharpened to exactly the same point.

'Is this for school?' Gabriel asked blankly.

'No, Gabriel, it's too good for that school of yours. This is for you to draw the fairy ring in Kerry and anything else that catches your eye here.'

Gabriel stared at the pad and then at his grandmother. Tears began to roll down the pale curve of his cheeks.

'No one's ever been that nice to me,' he said, 'not even Mum and Dad.'

She watched with pleasure how he ran his finger over the pages like an artist, noting their texture and thickness, then carefully closed the pad and hugged it to his narrow chest.

'Granny, can I keep it here, please?'

'It's yours, so you can do what you like with it.'

'It's just that I don't want Mum and Dad to tell me off for not doing my homework, and anyway, I don't want anyone to see my drawings.'

'Not even me?'

'Only you, Granny! And do you know what? I'm going to give you my first drawing.'

'Well, I can't wait for that, Gabriel. But tell me, hasn't your teacher seen how well you draw?'

Gabriel looked at her and the tears began to roll again.

'She doesn't let me draw because I have no coloured pencils.'

'What do you mean you haven't got any? I was with your mam when she bought them at the stationer's.'

'The other kids took them.'

'The fecking little bastards! And have you not told your teacher?'

'I can't, Granny. If I do, they gang up on me in the playground. The teacher thinks I've lost them, so she punishes me.'

'Good God almighty! Your mam told me you were always losing your school stuff. Have you not told her why?'

'No. I don't want her going to the teacher. Mum shouts a lot when she's angry. If the kids get punished because of me, they'll want to kill me. I don't want them to hate me even more, Granny. And please don't tell Mum and Dad. You won't, will you?'

The panic in Gabriel's eyes curbed her rising anger.

'Don't you worry. We'll find a way round this, child,' she said, and tapped her fingers on the pale oak table. Her heart was fluttering rapidly and she had to lean her forehead on the table.

'What's the matter, Granny? Granny? You've gone all white.' Gabriel gently removed her glasses which were lying askew on her left cheek.

'Bring me my pills from the cupboard behind you, the ones in the brown bottle, and some water,' she said in a flat, breathless voice.

Gabriel quickly did as he was bid. Cliona swallowed two pills and slowly revived.

'You're not going to die, are you?' he whispered, and clutched her hand.

'You can bet on your life I'm not going to do that for a long while,' she said, more worried about frightening her grandchild than the arrhythmia of her heart. 'I want to be around to see what you're up to! I just have to keep taking the pills.'

Later that day, Gabriel resolved that he would always remind her to take her pills, and he thought he wouldn't upset her with his stories about school; he would draw them instead. He couldn't imagine the bleak prospect of life without the haven his grandmother provided, nor the effortless understanding she showed of his inner world.

The following week Rosa rang unexpectedly; her calls usually fitted into a tight schedule – 9 p.m. Tuesdays and Thursdays were allotted to her mother – so Cliona felt a twinge of concern.

'Mum, there's a parent's meeting at the school tomorrow evening. Could you go for me? I've got to finish a project for work the next day and Daniel has another office meeting,' Rosa said.

Cliona smiled to herself when she detected the sheepish tone in her daughter's voice and thanked the luck of her Irish stars.

'Well, all right, but it's about time one of you two went to these meetings, useless as they are. I went to all of yours, you know.'

'Okay, Mum, don't start with your sermons. It starts at six, and don't forget to ask the teacher how Gabriel is doing. If you waste time talking to everybody after the meeting, she'll just slip out,' she said, her voice now ringing with impatience.

'You can be sure I won't,' Cliona said, and hung up gleefully.

***

Cliona's tired blue eyes observed the teacher and felt disheartened at the sight. She was in her late forties, wiry and desiccated. A brittle mass of greying corkscrew curls with blonde highlights bushed out over her shoulders. Frown lines were etched between her eyebrows and red lipstick sank into the creases around her thin lips. Her jaw, taut and belligerent, belied the otherwise delicate features, and no amount of hair could counteract its chiselled determination. Two unblinking brown marbles surveyed the chattering parents squashed into the children's chairs.

I bet she reads *New Developments in Education* in bed every night; fat lot of good it does her though, thought Cliona, and she struggled to repress an urge to rap loudly on the desk in front of her.

The teacher cleared her throat to address the parents in a loud, grating voice:

'Thank you all very much for coming. And please make sure you sign the attendance form which is being circulated. The reason for this rather impromptu meeting is to inform you that, due to recent concern about the cases of bullying that have been detected in many schools all over the country, we have invited a child psychologist to give talks to the pupils from the age of eight upwards. This is to make them aware of the devastating effects of bullying and to nip it in the bud, so to speak. The aim of the psychologist is to encourage children to speak openly about any cruelty from their classmates, and to dissuade any who are showing this tendency. Our school also offers guidance to parents who think their child may be a victim of bullying.'

Some of the parents looked at the teacher in horror whilst others began whispering to each other. Cliona raised her hand to speak but was waved down by Sra García, who continued, her voice louder still.

'And as an incentive to our pupils to increase their awareness of this most disturbing issue, we are holding an art competition for each age group. There will be a prize for the best drawing that expresses the anguish of being bullied, and the winner of each category will also take part in a regional competition on the same theme. The drawings will be carried out in the classroom to avoid any help at home! And please make sure your children bring their colouring pencils to class. The school will provide the sheets of paper.'

'Well, that's mighty generous of them,' Cliona said under her breath, and caught the eye of the woman sitting next to her, who nodded in agreement. Sra García glared at them and cleared her throat.

'I am pleased to say that in this class I have not detected any cases. They are, of course, only nine and ten years old! Nevertheless, it is always beneficial to open their eyes from an early age and discourage any signs.'

'As if she'd notice,' Cliona whispered, and repressed an urge to clear the phlegm from her throat. Sra García gave her audience a thin, tired smile.

'Due to lack of time I'm afraid that I'm unable to attend to parents' enquiries about their child's particular performance at this moment. Please do ask for an appointment if that is the case. Are there any questions?' Without even conceding five minutes of courtesy, Sra García thanked the now agitated parents for coming to the five-minute meeting, picked up her papers and proceeded to walk to the door.

'Ah, no you don't, you're not escaping me,' Cliona muttered to herself, and swiftly got up from her chair and blocked the door with her large frame.

'Sra García,' she said with a try at a sweet smile, 'I can see you're in a hurry and I don't want to inconvenience you in any way, but I have to talk to you for a moment.'

'Mrs O' Connell, if this is about Gabriel, I have just now said that an appointment has to be made. Perhaps your daughter could do that?' She looked at Cliona as if she were half-witted.

'I understood you perfectly, Sra García. It has nothing to do with Gabriel's performance, but rather with the drawing competition,' said Cliona, and taking advantage of her larger size, she propelled the teacher into the corridor. 'We can have a little more privacy here.'

'I am in a hurry. Just what is this about?' she said, shaking off Cliona's arm and turning to see if the other parents and grandparents were queuing behind. 'You had better walk with me to my car.'

'No problem, Sra García. I won't keep you two minutes.'

When they got to the teacher's black Citroën, Cliona opened her bag and took out a pack of twelve colouring pencils.

'These are for Gabriel, but I'm giving them to you so that you can keep them safely for him. Whenever you have a drawing class, and especially for the competition, I want you to make sure he has these pencils. Then he has to give them back to you. All right, Sra?'

'But this is ridiculous. At his age he has to look after his own property. He's always losing things as it is. He'll never learn this way,' she said with an air of resigned superiority.

'And have you never wondered if perhaps Gabriel doesn't lose them but has them taken from him? Have you never noticed how the other kids treat him?' Cliona said as icily as she could manage.

'Absolute nonsense. Nothing of what you're suggesting happens in my class. I should know. I spend five hours with them every day. And this would really be singling him out in front of the other children. And by the way, you really ought to control his language. The other day I actually heard him say 'fecking'. He was talking to himself in the playground, but it was loud enough for me to hear. I can't imagine who he's copied that from. Now, if you'll excuse me, I must be off. You can give the pencils to Gabriel your-self,' she said, and thrust the pack into Cliona's bag.

'Not so fast, Sra García. Your headmaster was an old colleague of my late husband's and often came to dinner at our house. I'm sure you wouldn't want him to suspect a case of overlooked bullying in your class now, would you?' she said, and firmly put the pencils on top of Sra García's pile of papers.

'Ah, and by the way, not a word of this to Gabriel's par-ents or to the kids in your class. I think you might be in for a surprise, Sra García.' Cliona patted her arm and then walked off, two bright pink spots in her cheeks, leaving the teacher, agape, slumped against her car and, Cliona felt acutely, boring holes of hatred into her departing back.

***

The following Thursday was a luminous spring day. The Mallorcan light, still without the aggressive glare of summer, distilled the purest essence from every colour it fell upon. The jacarandas lining the streets were in full bloom, and Gabriel picked up a few of the sticky bell-shaped flowers that covered the pavement. He dawdled on his way to his grandmother's and studied the rapidly withering flowers in his hand. He wondered how he could copy their shade of violet blue with the colouring pencils his grandmother had also given him.

'Well there you are, child. What took you so long to get here? The pasta will have congealed into a lump by now,' scolded Cliona with a smile on her face. 'And what was that tune you were humming? I've never heard it before!'

'Look at these flowers, Granny,' he said. 'I want to draw them but I haven't got this shade of blue. Do you think I could have my birthday present early? Could I have some paints? I won't ask for anything else, I promise.'

'Well now, let me think just how much some paints would cost,' said Cliona, frowning. 'I'll tell you what. I'll deduct the cost from your present for the day, but you must come with me to get them. I have no idea which ones to choose.'

Gabriel hugged his grandmother and buried his head in her warm breast, but not before having carefully placed the jacaranda flowers on the table.

'Do you know what, Granny? Today at school we did our drawing for the competition. We didn't have normal classes. A man came to explain what bullying was and we had to do a drawing about it. Sra García gave me some colouring pencils this time, a whole new pack just for me, but I had to give them back afterwards. Maybe she likes me more now.'

'Well, isn't that just great, Gabriel! And what did you draw?'

'I did a comic strip. It's got five parts.'

'Did you now? That must have been very difficult for such a young boy. Can you tell me what the story is?'

Gabriel was silent for a moment, and then spoke quietly.

'It's about me, Granny.'

***

Ten days later Cliona opened the door to Rosa, who had dropped by after picking Gabriel up from school. She walked briskly into the kitchen, her son trailing behind her. Cliona observed her daughter, who was dressed in elegant office clothes, her long black hair scraped up into a topknot which hardened her elfin features, and wondered how she could have produced someone so different to herself.

'Mum, you'll never guess what's happened,' she said, beaming at Gabriel, whose resemblance to his mother stopped at the physical.

'And what would that be, Rosa?' said her mother, annoyed at having been woken from her nap on the sofa where she had now spread herself out again.

'Gabriel's drawing has won the prize for his category and it's been entered for the regional competition! I never realised he could draw so well.'

Cliona quickly levered herself up and went into the kitchen.

'Come here, child,' she said, 'I'm going to hug you to death.'

'Have you seen the drawing, Rosa?' Cliona asked tentatively.

'Not yet. His teacher says there will be a little exhibition on Friday afternoon for the school open day. How did you know what to draw, Gabriel? I mean, it isn't easy to do a drawing about bullying, is it?'

Gabriel shrugged and looked at his grandmother.

'I want Granny to come on Friday too,' he said. 'She likes my drawings.'

'What drawings? I've never seen any at home,' said Rosa, eyeing her mother suspiciously.

'Gabriel draws with me on Thursdays, don't you, Gabriel? I've got a folder where I keep them. He's even copied my photo of Lough Brin. Do you want to have a look?'

'We must be going now. I'll have a look next time. Can't wait to tell Daniel! Come on, Gabriel, and stand up straight, will you?' she said as she clattered down the steps.

***

The exhibition was held in the school hall, which had a sickening smell of canteen dinners, disinfectant and musty paintwork. Flimsy wooden boards had been hastily erected, and stapled on them was the artwork produced over the year. One section was titled 'Prizewinning Drawings on the Theme of Bullying'. There were six drawings – one for each age group – but Gabriel's comic strip stood out dramatically from the other five. The parents contemplated it with expressions of discomfort and disbelief. They looked warily at Sra García and their own offspring, then left the hall, talking in whispers. Cliona waited until she could look at Gabriel's work by herself.

The first part of the comic strip showed a bleak school playground, reminiscent of a prison yard, with high walls and no vegetation. Outside the railings, parents were leaving in their cars or talking to each other as the children walked through the gates. The second was a corner of the playground. A dark-haired boy was being kicked and pinched by a group of five boys of the same age. But he wasn't fighting back; he was holding out his school bag to them with a look of quiet desperation. In the third, the boys had emptied his bag onto the ground. They were picking up his colouring pencils and putting them into their pockets. The fourth showed the classroom with its neat rows of tables and chairs. The children were at their desks, drawing in exercise books with colouring pencils. The teacher, a woman with stiff, curly hair, was looking angrily at the boy who had no colouring pencils on his table. He had his head down, but five boys were pointing and laughing at him. The fifth showed break-time in the playground. Some children were running, others were talking in groups, but the boy was eating his sandwich alone in the darkest corner. In the middle of the playground there were two teachers on duty standing close together, heads down, locked in conversation. The comic strip was drawn in stark strokes of black, white and grey. Only the pencils had vivid colours: the brightest red, blue, yellow, green, purple, pink and orange.

'Cliona! How nice to see you after all this time. Might I have a little word with you, away from this noise?' said a tanned, balding man in his sixties who looked like a suave entrepreneur in his immaculate lightweight suit.

Cliona turned from looking at the comic strip. She blinked back the tears and greeted Sr Marin, headmaster of her grandson's school.

'You have a very talented grandson, Cliona, and it looks as if he has exposed a case of bullying in this very school. Or is it just his imagination, I wonder?'

'Juan, I'm going to be perfectly clear,' said Cliona, who knew but didn't care if later her son-in-law called her an interfering old bag. 'This is Gabriel's story, don't you see? And if nothing is done about it, he won't be continuing in this school next year.'

Sr Marin did not lose his composure. He did have a master's in public relations, after all; but his mouth tightened and on his upper lip a few beads of sweat appeared. He looked across the hall at Sra García, who was milling with the parents and trying to look unperturbed by the sight of the headmaster talking to Cliona.

'Don't worry, Cliona. I'm going to be making a few changes in this school. But I do wish I'd been told before.' He turned and walked off briskly towards Rosa.

After the exhibition Rosa took Gabriel by the hand and led him out of the hall. Gabriel's comic strip and the headmaster's surprise at her lack of awareness of his suffering had shaken her deeply.

'I'm sorry, Gabriel. Why didn't you tell me? What can I do to put it right?'

'I want to go to Ireland with Granny to see the fairy ring. They'll put it right.'

Rosa sighed. 'Forget about the fairies, Gabriel. I'll put it right. Those kids won't bully you again. I'm going to talk to their parents personally and so will Sr Marin. And you could have asked me for the pencils and sketching paper. You never tell me anything. I am your mother, you know.'

'But you are always in a hurry and you're never pleased with me the way Granny is. Will you let me draw at home?' he asked anxiously.

'All right, all right, but homework first,' she said, and kissed the top of his head. Gabriel moved away quickly.

****

June arrived, and with it, the end of school. Gabriel's not very favourable school report was mitigated by the news that he had won the regional drawing competition. His parents, informed of his exceptional artistic ability, were advised to allow him to attend free drawing classes for children at the official School of Art in the city. It took a while for their practical minds to find a use for this in Gabriel's future, but they eventually accepted in the hope

that it would turn him into a 'normal, sociable child', and
not make him an arty freak. His grandmother championed
his cause with all the passion of her absolute belief in him.

'Mother of God, Rosa, you haven't got an ordinary child
there, you've got an extraordinary one. Stop wanting him to
be like all the others and give him the space he needs to
develop. He needs to get away from Mallorca for a while to
recover. Our little trip to Ireland will do him the world of
good, don't you know?'

'All right, Mother, but make sure you don't feed him
more tales of fairy rings. He's nearly ten, for Christ's sake.
And will you please stop swearing in front of him!'

***

Gabriel speared a dumpling in his stew and eyed it
suspiciously.

'What's this? Don't you have spaghetti in Ireland?' he
asked his great uncle Rory, who was ladling large amounts
of stew into his plate.

'Now, you have to try a good Irish stew,' Rory said,
beaming at him. 'None of that foreign muck in my house.
You look as though you need building up, my boy. If you
spent a few days with me, I'd soon put some colour in your
cheeks.'

Gabriel and Cliona had arrived in Dublin on the first of
July. Gabriel was impressed by two things above all: the dark
grey stone of the buildings, whose cold, damp texture
seeped into his fingers as he caressed the walls that turned
black in the rain; and the warmth and friendliness of the
people who smiled and talked to him as if he were the most
fascinating child in town. He wondered how the dank buildings and the predominant grey layer of cloud could produce

21

such cheerful inhabitants. No one must feel lonely here, he thought.

They stayed just one night in Rory's spacious architect-designed flat. Cliona's hospitable elder brother also lent them his car for the journey to County Kerry. He had mapped out their journey to Lough Brin in minute detail. She was well aware of how much he doubted her navigational abilities, which she also did, but when he offered to drive them she refused as gently as she could.

'It just has to be me and the child, Rory. I'll explain later,' she said to her large, kindly brother. She felt a pang of guilt because she knew how much this solitary man had been looking forward to their company, and she knew, too, that he was too sensitive to her needs to insist. She watched how he covered his disappointment by making stacks of sandwiches and checking the car for the journey. And she thought it was time she made more visits to Dublin.

Cliona and Gabriel rose early the next morning. The Dublin air was fresh and sharp and woke in both their hearts the magic of hope, of endless possibility. While Cliona loaded the car with food and rucksacks she felt her heart expand with a rush of euphoria, just as when she was a child filled with some marvellous expectation. She, too, was about to discover the magical land which lay behind the photograph that had captivated her decades ago. The framed image in her living room was the wild heart of Ireland, which over the years was fading in her memory. Her grandson was leading her back, back to the dark pool of her beginnings, to the rediscovery of who she was before life in Mallorca blurred the edges of her Irish soul.

'Be careful with my rucksack, Granny. I've got a special box in it,' Gabriel said, his face white with excitement, 'and don't forget your pills.'

'Don't you worry about that. Nothing will happen to your box. Now sit back and just enjoy the scenery. We're on our way to Killarney, where we'll spend the night, and then next day off to Lough Brin. And have no fear; your grandmother will be guided by the travelling fairies!'

'Have you ever seen a fairy, Granny?'

'Well, I thought I saw one when I was a girl. It had lovely translucent wings and a cheeky face. But it might have been my imagination.' She watched Gabriel open his mouth in astonishment. Then she began to chant:

'Come away, O human child!
To the woods and waters wild,
With a fairy hand in hand,
For the world's more full of weeping than
You can understand.'

Gabriel sat on the edge of his seat. 'Go on, Granny, I like it! What is it?'

'It's from a poem called "The Stolen Child" by a famous Irish poet called Yeats. I can't remember any more. I'll find it for you when we get home. Now, settle back. We'll have to stop and look at the map sometimes. You'll have to help me with that, Gabriel. Your uncle Rory thinks we may get lost, but we'll show him, won't we!'

They eventually arrived in the town of Killarney in the evening after a few wrong turns and much poring over the map. They ambled along the narrow streets looking for the hostel Rory had booked them into. It was near St Mary's

Cathedral. Gabriel looked in awe at its structure. Built of brown and grey stone, its stark beauty was enhanced by a background of lakes and mountains which beckoned him to wander in fearless freedom. He thought of the gothic cathedral of Mallorca, hemmed in by the sea and the ancient walls of the city, magnificent but static. But this windswept cathedral somehow invited him to movement, to exploration, to discovery of what lay beyond.

He observed the buildings in the small town centre as they walked along the narrow streets, and thought he could easily live there. There was nothing grand about them with their red, cream and brown façades; they were homely, welcoming edifices, unlike the towering blocks that intimidated him in Palma. His grandmother told him that many of them were guest houses offering rest and grounding to travellers overwhelmed from exploring the wild beauty of the surrounding countryside. He, too, was beginning to feel overwhelmed, so when Cliona asked him if he wanted to explore further before settling in the hostel, Gabriel, now locked tightly inside himself, said he preferred to do that on the way back. First he had to see the fairy ring. At that moment he just wanted to have supper and go to bed so that morning would come quickly.

By nine o'clock he and his grandmother were lying in the creaking double bed that was wedged into their minute room. Gabriel counted the cracks in the flaking white paint of the ceiling for a while and imagined what lay before him the next day. He waited for Cliona to fall asleep, and when he was certain she had, he got up and opened his box. He fingered the contents and when satisfied, put it carefully back into his backpack. Then he curled up beside his grandmother and was eventually lulled into sleep by the rhythm of her gentle snores.

Gabriel was woken by the dawn chorus and the first trickle of light coming through the threadbare curtains.

'Granny, Granny, are you awake?' he whispered and gave her a prod.

'Well, by Jesus, I am now,' she moaned.

'Let's go then, Granny. I can't wait any longer. Please!'

'All right, all right, hold your horses, Gabriel. We'll have to take a packed breakfast. No one is up at this unholy hour, that's for sure.'

Dawn was just breaking as they got into the car with their rucksacks. A few wisps of rose-gold cloud softened the emerging sun that picked out the heavy dew on tightly packed rooftops and ghost-tale lamp posts.

'We're going to have good weather, Gabriel. It's only an hour's drive; we'll soon be there,' she said, and hoped it wouldn't be too much for her frail-looking grandson who was pale with overexcitement.

They drove out through the town, silent except for the occasional dog barking or the chirruping birds. They travelled through the rugged countryside, the long grass tossing and glistening with damp, and soon they were nearing Lough Brin. The lake sat in an austere valley at the foothills of the green, almost bare slopes of low mountains: the McGillycuddy Reeks, Cliona told Gabriel. As they approached, they could see Lough Brin to the left, a tranquil lake lit in places by the hazy sun. And in the centre of their view, on a grassy mound, stood a solitary hawthorn in full white flower, framed on either side by the mountains. There

were no other trees in sight, just shrubs and mossy boulders
dotted randomly.

'Look!' Gabriel said, pointing at the hawthorn encircled
by a halo of light as it momentarily shaded the sun. 'Just like
in your photo!'

'Holy Mother of God, if it isn't just the same!' exclaimed
Cliona. 'We chose the right day, didn't we?'

Cliona parked the car on a bridle path at the foot of the
hill and they began their ascent, Cliona's backpack filled
with breakfast, Gabriel's with his little plywood box and
sketch pad. Cliona puffed up the slope, but Gabriel ran on
until he reached the hawthorn.

'Will you not wait a while, Gabriel?' Cliona called. 'I'm
sixty not ten, you know. The pills can't change that.'

Gabriel, transfixed, didn't answer, but he kept a respect-
ful distance from the tree. He had taken the box from his
backpack and was holding it like an offering.

'Now isn't that the most precious sight,' said Cliona
when she finally stood panting next to her grandson. 'And I
have to thank you, Gabriel, for bringing me here. This is a
gift for both of us, you know. But now let's sit down and
have a drink. My heart is nearly coming out of my mouth!'

'Wait a moment, Granny. I have to do something first.'

Gabriel walked slowly up to the ring of boulders, knelt
down and opened the box. From it he took out some olives,
some white stones and a sheet of paper.

'What have you got there?' said Cliona, coming up behind him.

It was a drawing of her olive tree with a circle of small,
irregular-shaped stones around the base of the trunk.

'This is a gift from Mallorca for the fairies,' Gabriel said
with solemnity, and he placed the olives, stones and drawing

inside the ring of boulders. Then he closed his eyes and whispered, 'Hello fairies. We have no fairy rings in Mallorca so I made a pretend one in my granny's garden, like the one in my drawing. Would any of you like to go there to make real ones? I would make sure no one hurt you, and you could sing and dance forever under the pines and olive trees.'

Cliona took Gabriel's hand and they both knelt on the rough grass, a fresh breeze rustling the branches of the hawthorn and only the faint sounds of humming insects and distant bird cries over the lake breaking the silence.

After a while Gabriel said in a low voice, 'Granny, Granny, the fairies spoke to me. They said they would prefer to stay in Ireland because this is their home, but that if I concentrated very hard, I'd be sure to see a Mallorcan fairy in the woods there. And they said if I ever needed help, I only had to call them and they would protect me. And do you know, Granny, they told me I should keep drawing, because one day I would be a great painter and no one would ever laugh at me again.'

Cliona embraced Gabriel. 'And they are right, my child. They will be your protectors all your life because you have a pure heart and can see and draw what others can't.'

Gabriel gently slipped out of his grandmother's hug and went up to the fairy ring. Then, without warning, he stepped inside. He walked around counting the paces: one, two, three, four ... Then he sat on a boulder and ran his fingers with great tenderness along the curves and edges of the stone. After a while he stepped out the circle and went to sit by Cliona, who was spreading a cloth for their breakfast.

'Mother of Divine Grace, I was wondering if you'd disappeared with the Little People!' she exclaimed and handed him a chocolate spread sandwich.

Satiated with pure air and quiet joy, they ate their sandwiches in silence under the pale canopy of early morning. Both would return to that sacred hour in the coming years; it never dimmed in their memory.

When Cliona was packing away the remains, Gabriel said, 'Don't let's go yet, Granny. I want to draw the fairy ring. I've brought my sketching pad.'

Cliona lay on her back and watched a beetle run up an open blade of grass, while Gabriel sketched and rubbed out until he was satisfied with a final rendering of the fairy ring. She was in a deep state of reverie, her body moulding to the soil and roots beneath, when Gabriel's voice pulled her out of her daydreams.

'Look, I've finished!'

Inside the ring he had drawn a circle of smiling fairies in colourful suits and dresses; no wings, just Little People, and in the middle of the circle was himself, no taller than them, drawing pad in his hand.

'Granny, the fairies are my friends, the only friends I have apart from you. When I'm grown up, I'm going to build a house here and I'll spend all day painting and looking. Will you come with me?'

'Don't you know I'll always be with you, Gabriel,' she said, and lay back on the grass.

The Last Months
of
Violet Koski

Seaford, England, 2015

November

They've brought me to this place from the hospital. I thought I was going home, but no, I've ended up in 'the best nursing home in town,' so they tell me, 'and it's only a short distance from your own house, dear.' I know the street. The sea is there at the bottom of it. I used to go past this home on the bus. And now I'm in it. It's not that it's not quite nice; the room looks onto shrubs and trees, from what I can see. But it's November, dark November, and not much light is getting into the cracks of my poor old retina, eaten away like a mouse has been nibbling at it all these years till it's like an Emmental cheese, with more holes than substance to be of any use.

I can make out a wardrobe next to the armchair where they've left me sitting, too exhausted to make the slightest move. It's much too small for all the clothes I have at home. Alice says she'll bring me some of my prettiest tops and jumpers. But what use have I of anything pretty here? What remains of my quickly waning vanity will certainly disappear in this room. Because that is what I'm reduced to: a room. I'm being stripped away. Before, it was little by little, but now it's speeding up, getting down to the bare essentials: a couple of nightdresses, my knickers, vests. No bras; what's the point? They only dig into my bony back, and my once pride and joy still hang round my waist, however hard I try and pack them into those ridiculously small cups (what was Alice thinking when she bought them?) They just slide out like two slippery eels, all long and skinny. Is that a TV on the top of a chest of drawers in front of the window? Not much good to me now. At home I can sit right up to the edge of my set. They placed my armchair at just the right angle so that if I looked sideways, I could catch a few images on the screen. I can't do that here. Something else I'm stripped of: my armchair and my TV.

Alice came today. I was so pleased to see her, I had a little cry. She has chosen my best jumpers and shown them to me before folding them and putting them in the drawers, all neat and tidy. She hung a couple of jackets and trousers in the wardrobe, bustling around with her usual energy. Then she said, 'Look, Violet, I've brought your favourites. Which one do you want to wear today?' I made an effort, just for her, and I picked out anything because really I can see much less than she or other people think. Pride has made me a good actress, although maybe everyone goes along with my play-acting. But the truth is that I don't care what I wear anymore; I don't care what my hair looks like, even though Alice does it so well. I cared, a bit, when I could choose what to wear myself and I was still able to rake a comb through my sparse hair in an effort to make it stand up, peering into the magnifying mirror in my bedroom and then squinting out of the window, trying to make out what the garden looked like and feeling triumphant if I could just glimpse a bush. I'd be pacified by hearing the birds or if the odd ray of sunlight burst through, because I knew it was all there. And I would count the days till spring when I'd be able to sit out under the cherry tree, just close my eyes and listen to the sparrows or the pair of blackbirds that come back to nest every year. I'd enjoy having a moan at the squawking seagulls and at the noise the schoolchildren made on the playing field nearby; or when I could listen to the afternoon play under the falling blossom, teacup slurping tea onto my trousers.

They tell me there's a beautiful garden at the back of the nursing home, and when the weather's better, they'll wheel me outside. But I just want my own garden. I don't want to be taken outside for an airing with all the other inmates. When I was brought here, I could make out some kind of rabbit's warren; lots of little rooms, cubby holes, nooks and crannies where you'd least expect them. How many of us are crammed in here, for God's sake? It's not that isn't pleasant enough – nice soft furnishings, and colours – but I'd promised myself I'd never go into one of these places. It made me go all cold just to think about it, so how has it happened? How did I get manoeuvred into this? Did I agree at some point in the hospital when I was so under the wheels, so near the end, that I just gave up? Surely not. That's not me. I was always a quiet little fighter. I'd like to blame someone; it would make it easier, but in the end I can only accuse this rotting body which won't do what I tell it to. And it's not that I haven't eked out my energy very pre-cisely. A little here, a little there, so I don't collapse. My mind controlled it all. I carefully existed, careful not to fall, careful not to get burnt, careful to take my pills, counting them out twice a day. Some of them got lost down the side of the chair, it's true, but most times I got it right. So how come head and body are not coordinating any more, and I'm stuck in this uncomfortable armchair waiting for the nurse to come and help me into the airbed and bring me a cup of tea? I could cry, but they're not going to see it. Maybe if they

notice I have my wits about me, they'll let me go home soon.
Maybe.

I must admit that my experience of sleeping in an airbed
is very positive. My back doesn't hurt so much. It's like being on a sea, the waves gently rippling, up and down, side to
side. Sometimes it makes strange noises when it fills. It's the
nearest I'm going to get to floating on the sea. Ah, the sea;
so near, it's only at the bottom of this road, but so far now.
I'll never again lie on the stony beach and watch the blue-
green water shimmering in the sun, nor feel its icy embrace
on my shivering skin. How I long for the sea. Yes, I know,
I must be grateful. Later on, they'll wheel me to the front
and I'll feel the breeze, smell the air of that proletarian sea,
as my daughter Annie once called it. For it's a working-class
sea, with no tourists, just the odd ferry crossing the channel
and solitary walkers throwing stones for their dogs. But I
can't see it or touch it. I'll pretend. I'll say, 'Oh yes, it's quite
calm today,' just so my companion will feel better. Come to
think of it, I've spent half my life telling little lies or half-
truths so other people will feel better. Now I can't hide from
the truth facing me; neither can I hide under the blankets,
as I did in my childhood when I didn't like what the world
was throwing at me.

A girl came in and pulled the curtains, early in the morning. All bright and breezy, as they are in these places, she
asked, 'Would you like a cup of tea, Violet?'

'No, I wouldn't, it's still night, you fool.' I'd like to say it,
but I don't because I'm still nice, easy-going Violet who's
always polite and no trouble at all.

So I asked, 'What time is it?' It's six thirty. My God, is it going to be like this every day? I said yes to tea and didn't drink it.

They come and go, shower me, bring me pills, food and tea, anything I want. I can't make out who they are yet. They're always changing. I want to say sharply, 'Stand in front of me so I can see you. Tell me your name.' But as usual, I don't want to bother them and so I put up with a confusion that saddens me day by day.

How long is this going on for? I really can't be doing with it, I really can't. What can I look forward to? What's left?

I know. I'll make sure I get to Christmas. I'll ask the girls to spend it with me at home. Surely, they'll let me out then? Yes, I'm determined to get to Christmas. Alice can make a list of things to get like every year, except this time it'll be the last one.

What will I do all day? I can listen to the radio if someone will tune it, or to the CD talking books Alice brought from home. I can still more or less make out where the start button is. Trouble is, I keep falling asleep in the middle and then I don't know where I am and can't put the damned thing back to where it was. And I'm not going to ask the nurse again. I don't want to be a nuisance and keep ringing the bell like the others do. I think they must keep pressing out of sheer spite. When I think about it, and I do a lot of that, it's the first time in my long life that I've been seriously thwarted. I've always had my own way in the end, through little ingenious manoeuvres that I've been quite proud of. But nothing and no one is going to get me out of here. I've been sentenced to a loss of independence. I feel so angry with myself. I shouldn't have signed those bloody papers. How can I get out?

I spoke to Carol and Annie on the phone. 'You'll get used to it, Mum. It's really a nice place, the best one, and you know you can't manage on your own now.' But what do they know? I know I'm not going to get used to it. I'll die in this rabbit hole. And I'm not going to hide what I feel from them this time. I'll moan, even it makes them feel bad. If I had the energy, I'd shout out my anger and woe, but I must keep my strength. The truth is I just want to be with my girls. They're the closest to the bone. No matter the arguments and disappointments, they're dearest to my heart. It's funny how you forget or don't care about what went wrong. I just want to have them near. That's the crux of it. When you are stripped of the layers of mistakes and resentment, successes and failures, of how angry you got at one time or how joyful you were at one point; when you get rid of the frustration at them for not turning out exactly how you wanted, or because they didn't like you as much as you thought you deserved, then all you feel is a pure flame of love that was burning there all the time under the debris. Of course, they don't understand that. They're still trying to figure me out as a mother, with my good and dark side; they haven't got the whole picture yet and they might never.

But then there's Tim. How long has it been now? Thirty, forty years? He'd be in his sixties, an old man. I can't quite remember what he looks like and sometimes I don't think of him for weeks on end. Because I don't like myself when I think of him. YOU ARE A FAILURE is written on my mental screen in big red letters whenever he pops up. Everyone felt sorry for me when he disappeared, and of course everyone knew it was his father's fault with all that bullying, nothing to do with me. I was such a quiet little mouse, anything for an easy life, and there was no crossing Douglas otherwise I would have been on the receiving end. And I did need people to like me back then. But we all have a dark side, don't we? Tim always knew how to bring out the worst in me; he made me feel uncomfortable, or should I say guilty? So in the end it was easier to ignore him. But there's a sharp little stone wedged in the centre of my heart that never shifts.

My room is next to the kitchen, so I get all the smells wafting in and I can hear the constant banging about and clattering of plates. I also get snippets of their young people's chatter about where they've been, where they're going and who they're meeting; that excitement over just the fact of living which a good body and circulation give you. What a gift youth is, and how unaware we are of it! But I don't begrudge it. Hearing them makes this place feel less like the antechamber to a morgue. I like the way they pop their heads round the corner and ask if I want anything. They stand there so firmly rooted. They don't sway like I do; they aren't nearly blown over by gusts of wind or toppled by crowds. I am almost uprooted; the sapless trunk is waving side to side and I must be supported by strong hands that dig into my papery flesh. If only I could see their faces, instead of a faint blur. And I wish there weren't so many nurses and sisters. I have to concentrate to remember who they are, and sometimes I give up. I tell myself, 'Violet, you're in the best nursing home, you're given what you like to eat, and nobody forces you to finish it. They shower you gently and only help you to dress if you want. You're privileged.' I still fumble my way to the toilet next to the room because I refuse to sit on the commode that's waiting ominously next to the bed.

Today Alice took me to have lunch in the dining room here. She had to push me in the wheelchair as I only have breath for two or three steps. I peered into the other rooms on the way. They are artificially cosy with photographs on the chests of drawers trying to imitate some kind of sitting room back home. Alice has brought photos for my room too and one of Gabriel's paintings that I liked, maybe because of the story that went with it. I'll ask Alice to tell me the story again later. We had our chicken lunch; well, at least she did. I just had a mouthful. I haven't been hungry for a long time. My back aches when I'm sitting up, so Alice wheeled me to my room. What hit me then was the smell of urine half concealed under air fresheners, an undeniable waft of stale pee along the corridor. All those pads on poor wasted bottoms. I will not wear pads, not even at the end. I solemnly swear to myself that I will not succumb to that indignity. It's the last bastion of my independence. I was exhausted and had to go back to bed.

'You'll get to know the others if you go to the communal lounge,' Alice encouraged me while making me comfortable. But I can't be bothered. The only thing we have in common is that we've lost our homes, our lives, our illusions. Some have lost their minds, too. At least that hasn't happened to me. My body is crumbling away like I'm losing bits every day, but my brain is as active as ever. I can't sleep with all those thoughts and memories rolling around.

Sometimes I feel like snapping their heads off when they come in and talk to me in their little voices: 'All right, dear?' as if I were half-witted. Of course I'm not all right. Would you be if you were suddenly shunted, albeit gently, into a box of a room and were asked stupid questions all day long? I bet I'm better read than the lot of you. Just because I'm ninety-three, have heart failure, severe macular degeneration, and weigh under six stone, doesn't mean to say I don't have thoughts and feelings that rise up as strong as anyone's.

I suppose I'll end my days here. I wonder what it's like, death. It's beginning to lose its grim countenance. In fact, it's starting to have an inviting smile. People talk about the tunnel, and I used to think it was because of the cells breaking down. But I had my own experience in the hospital just a month ago. I nearly went over to the other side; I was so ill with pneumonia. I put my head back one night in agonising pain and there it was, rather like the tunnel you see down at the underground. Near the end was a tall figure slumped against the wall as if it was tired of waiting. I couldn't see the face. But then an oxygen mask was clamped over my mouth and an injection sent me off to sleep. So I suppose I shouldn't worry; someone's waiting there to give me a hand into the other world. Could it be Douglas? It didn't look like him, but he would definitely be tired of waiting. I can hear him saying, 'About time, too. What have you been doing? I've been stuck here for ages.'

Alice is here again to keep me company. She's a social worker now but she used to be a teacher. She spends most of her free time with me, especially as Gabriel is often away in Oxford, teaching. He's a guest professor of art at Balliol this year but he comes down to Seaford as much as he can. Then we both lighten up. My best friend, Joy, was Alice's mother. She died a year ago and I think I'm a kind of substitute for Alice; not that I'm much fun in my present state.

But she and Gabriel have taken me on, and they ease the loneliness. My girls are so far away.

How Alice ended up marrying a Mallorcan with Irish blood is quite a story, but it all stems from the painting of the fountain which she has leant on the wall above the chest of drawers. When I feel stronger, I'll go and peer at it. But I'm tired now, so I'll just lie back and remember the story. Alice will fill in any gaps.

The Fountain

Palma de Mallorca, 1998

It's not an eye-catching fountain. Quite the opposite. You'd walk by, giving a cursory glance at its unadorned yellowy-grey stone and the spindly flow of water rising up and trickling down into the polished basin. If you happened to wander into the small Venetian-style square where the fountain sits in its centre, you'd be more impressed by the buildings that overlook it. For you have come into what was once part of the sacred heart of the city. On one side looms the once thriving seminary, rather ominous and prison-like with its narrow windows giving onto the cobbled square. A couple of students can still be spotted diligently studying in their austere rooms. Opposite the seminary are old buildings converted into tiny apartments, too tightly packed together for lifts. The inhabitants of these modest dwellings seem to be imbued with the same monastic energy that still lingers on in the square; there are no families, no lively children, no one under forty. They are single and appear to have chosen the square as a kind of retreat. There are a couple of painters, a musician, a composer, an eighty-four-year-old woman who holds the keys to the church, and others who need to be by themselves for a time, the lonely wanderers and observers of life. The shutters or billowing curtains at their windows are at the same time disturbing and comforting in the quiet. The far end of the square is almost entirely taken up by the back wall of St Jerome's church, seventeenth century baroque style, now in disuse and crumbling. The other end is open and leads to shady little streets near the ancient Jewish quarter, and further on, deep into the dark entrails of the city.

Alice has recently rented one of the little apartments. Hers is one of billowing curtains as she likes to spend time watching the fountain and observing the only lit-up room in the seminary in front of her. She imagines how it must have been in more pious times: the feverish activity of eager students crossing the square and poring over their books into the small hours; when the whole area was a place of erudition, mysticism and multicultural exchange, with Jewish cartographers and *Iuliano* philosophers vying for space and time. Now the most numerous inhabitants are the doves that wait on the rooftop of the seminary for the water to be turned on in the fountain. This happens punctually at nine in the morning, and just as punctually it is turned off at nine at night. Fifteen minutes before the water rises in the fountain, they swoop down and wait patiently in the basin to drink the cool morning water and refresh their feathers. When the clocks are put forward in the autumn, they come and wait at quarter to eight and won't move for an hour until the water comes, as if their day can't begin without their bath.

But they are not the only users of the fountain. Alice has spent hours watching the visitors. She is still waiting for the new term to begin at the institute and likes to while away her time observing her new whereabouts. Leaning over her tiny balcony to catch the breeze at the end of an extremely hot Mediterranean summer, she watches and waits. There is nothing dignified, sanctimonious or wise about the few visitors. Some are curious, sweating tourists wandering into this relic of long-gone solemnity on their way to visiting the

Jewish quarter and the magnificent, lightless churches further on. At weekends, sometimes children come and fill
their water pistols; the shrill cries of their joyous battles
pierce the drowsy square and rudely awaken it. Then, just as
quickly as they appeared, they disappear, leaving a trail of
water on the cobbles and an empty silence broken now and
then by the cooing of the doves. In the early morning a few
drug addicts and homeless come. They use the fountain to
wash their hands and faces before stumbling off to secluded
corners in which to sleep or collapse. The unwanted ones,
the dregs, sit at the same fountain where the most holy and
the wisest of society conversed about morality and God.
Now, in the late afternoon at the main entrance to the
square, a discreetly parked van belonging to the Red Cross
offers methadone to the less hopeless.

Alice has noticed a girl in her twenties. She is the first to
arrive in the morning when nobody is yet about. She washes
her underwear in the fountain with a small piece of soap and
puts the wet clothes into a plastic bag. She uses the same
soap to wash her gaunt face and splashes water on her hair.
Then she goes to the nearest car parked at the entrance to
the square and combs her hair, looking into the side mirror.
When she is satisfied, she takes a bottle of baby cologne
from her rucksack and rubs some into her hair and neck.
She puts it away with care, her treasured possession, and sits
down on a bench. She has the look of the wolf about her,
the eyes furtive and distrustful, used to abuse and misuse,
always ready for flight. She has the hunger of the wolf about
her, too, and the cunning of the survivor. Her clothes are
grubby and stained, but her clean face and sweet-smelling
hair give her the right to sit on the bench and watch, Alice
likes to think. In her romantic musings, Alice imagines she

is almost beyond hope, but she won't give up the freedom of the streets. Her loneliness is absolute, and sitting on the bench, she has a Zen-like detachment which no master could ever teach her. She lives each day as it comes, no future and an erased past; nothing to clutch onto, just what the here and now bring her.

Alice watches her every day. Sometimes the girl comes across a few colleagues. There is solidarity among them and playfulness. They joke and stumble about, arms around each other, then each one is off, alone. She always does her ablutions when no one is around, in her one moment of privacy, her one moment of intimate dignity. She has turned and looked up at Alice, who likes to think she has felt her gentle gaze upon her and seen the compassion in her eyes, that she is waiting for the moment to help her. But underneath that fantasy, Alice senses the girl has smelt her fear and perceived the shame she battles with, how horror overcomes her goodwill, and that, above all, she is a challenge to all the lofty ideals Alice has nurtured and defended.

But one evening Alice decides that the next morning she will invite her into her apartment. She'll say: 'Come upstairs and take a shower in my bathroom.' She'll smile at her, all light and confidence, and the girl will smile back and humbly take up her offer. Then maybe she'll offer her some breakfast. At first she'll be timid, but then gradually she'll open up and will start talking about her life and how she got into such dire times. Alice imagines how each morning there will be the ritual of the shower, breakfast and conversation. A strange friendship will grow between them, and Alice will even persuade her to get help to overcome her addiction …

Alice is up early next morning. She has slept in fits and starts and is stiff with unease. The girl arrives at the fountain at her usual time and begins to take out her soap and the plastic bag with the underwear. Alice is watching her from the window, her mouth dry and speechless with fear. She is plucking up courage to call out to her when the girl looks up at her defiantly, the wolf ready to snarl. And Alice perceives that the sixth sense of the wolf knows what she would like to say, can smell her fear. Instead of help, she senses a trap. 'Another of those bloody do-gooders trying to get me into an institution over a cup of coffee,' Alice is certain she is thinking. Under the force of the girl's stare Alice feels despised and suddenly inferior. She lowers her eyes. The girl picks up her soap and clothes, stuffs them quickly into her rucksack and, with a glare at Alice, leaves the square. No ablutions for her today.

Although Alice is ashamed, she is also secretly relieved. She moves away from the window and slumps into the chair. She has tried to suppress her own instinct, which was screaming: 'Don't let her into your house. You don't know what she's capable of. She may rob you with a knife at your throat. She may bring all the other druggies with her another day. And you only wanted to help *her*, didn't you? Because she's a young girl and you felt sorrier for her than the others. But she's no different to the rest. She's crossed over into a different territory and you don't have the map.'

Alice admits she is not ready to cross those boundaries yet. However hard she has worked on herself, however 'enlightened' she thought she was, she has to accept defeat. Her instinctual sense of self-preservation, that primordial fear, has risen out of the same dark pit as everyone else's. Miss altruism is at bottom no better than the despised self-seeking rest, she realises, not without a lingering self-pity.

***

The school year has begun and there is less time for gazing from the window. She hardly looks at the girl now, who still comes every morning. Her pupils are her main concern. And soon she will be moving from the square. The apartment has served its purpose. Now it is too small and cramped and she has an imperious need to get away. She has already found a bigger, more modern apartment away from the city centre, with good sea views. Her time is taken up with teaching, thinking about her students and their difficulties. She likes her job as assistant English language teacher. She makes sure her self-esteem is kept buoyant by becoming popular with her pupils, although that isn't difficult – a young, blonde, foreign newcomer who makes the classes fun is the dream of every baccalaureate student, especially the male ones.

The day arrives for the removal of her few boxes. It's a bright October morning, a luminous autumn day, the early sunlight squinting into the square. The doves are waiting at the fountain, undisturbed by passers-by on this quiet Saturday morning. The water is turned on, and as usual they refresh their wings and drink. Then suddenly there is a flap, and they are up again on the seminary rooftop. Alice looks out to see what has frightened them. Coming up to the fountain is the girl. She is with two men, one in a wheelchair. They position the wheelchair in front of the fountain. Then she takes out an old can of shaving foam and a razor from her rucksack. She begins to shave the man in the wheelchair, tapping and rinsing the razor in the fountain. She takes her time, shaving with care until she is satisfied with the result. Then she gives the razor and the can to the other man, who starts to shave himself. The man in the wheelchair wipes his face with his shirt. They don't talk to each other. Everything is done slowly and with great calm. When they are finished, they go off together. Half an hour later the girl is back by herself. She carries out her routine, washing her underwear and then her face and hair. She looks into the side mirror of the nearest car and applies the cologne. Tired from so much effort, she rests her frail body on the bench and closes her eyes. After fifteen minutes she is off again, wandering into the dark alleys.

Alice closes the shutters and the windows. There is a dull heaviness in her heart that she struggles to ignore. She sits on one of the boxes and waits for a long while before phoning a friend to come and take her to her new apartment. The initial excitement she felt when she climbed the narrow stairway for the first time has now become a dull monotony. Alice hasn't conversed with the old lady for a while although she knows how she looked forward to her small quota of attention, to the tea and biscuits she would prepare for Alice in her tiny kitchen. She has been her main source of information about the history of the square and for little snippets of gossip about the locals. Alice sensed that nobody had asked her before she arrived. And her guilty conscience tells her that she has retired into her poky ground-floor flat and church duties, into the lonely routine she nearly dared to think belonged to the past.

Neither has Alice got to know the other inhabitants of the square, who at first she imagined the jealous guardians of an almost mystical knowledge, of a secret enlightenment only revealed to a chosen few. All she got out of them was a perfunctory *'Bon dia'*. Most days they just scuttle past one another, hoping they won't have to greet anyone. 'Don't come into my world, I don't want to go into yours, either' says the half-smile on the stairway. Their self-imposed retreat might have improved their painting or composing, but it has had a dire effect on their humanity. They have sallow, papery skins and a drabness which comes from sitting inside four walls for hours and hours. Their blood has pooled at their feet, the brains devoid of vitality and nourishment. A good slap on the back of the neck is what's needed there. Get that sluggish circulation back into their heads, Alice imagines with some spite. They no longer watch the morning and evening spectacle of the doves, nor wonder about each other. The drug addicts and homeless of the square could teach them a lesson in companionship, Alice has thought many a time. What is it about this place? she wonders, sitting hunched up on the biggest box. Do all the inhabitants end up having the life sucked out of them, as if they were the ghosts of their medieval ancestors? She could see parts of them falling away day by day; these poor ossified beings, gradually disintegrating into the ancient walls.

A few days ago a new guy moved into the apartment above hers. He is about her age, twenty-five, tall, thin and black-haired. Another painter, she thought, as she saw him struggling up the narrow stairway with an easel. Alice was surprised when he greeted her in Mallorcan. From the whiteness of his skin she assumed he was somewhere from the north. Well, he'll soon fit in with the rest of them, she thought, and dismissed him.

Alice remembers when she first arrived on the island from England. It was August; the humidity and heat was at its highest, and getting off the plane was like walking into a bowl of warm soup. But the smell of pine resin pervading the air, the unique light spangling the sea, bouncing off concrete and harshly revealing ugly corners and spectacular bougainvillea on white buildings, soon penetrated every blood cell. Nothing escaped that hard sun. Like a giant torch beam in the high Mediterranean sky, it searched out and captured all flaws in minute detail but also enhanced every form of beauty till the overwhelmed beholder could take in no more and had to turn away. Houses and apartments were shuttered against it, particularly in the old quarters of the city whose dark, narrow streets seemed to defend themselves against the assailant. The mountain range to the north-west of the island offered some respite to the villages scattered through its valleys. The air was fresher there and temperatures two or three degrees lower, as Alice discovered on her hikes. Soon she felt privileged to be in this one-time paradise where everything was close at hand: the sea, mountains, unspoilt villages and stretches of yellowy-green countryside spattered mostly with carob, olive and almond trees and the red, tilled earth that yielded excellent potatoes. The exploited coastal areas were forgotten when you found the paths leading into a physical heaven just half an hour from Babel's Tower and the modern tourist machinery. And the city itself: ancient, suspicious and wily, used to waves of invaders over the centuries, forced to accommodate all and trusting none. It had been and, in a sense, still was a Phoenician port of importance where money was god, although the abundance of imposing churches would have you thinking otherwise.

When Alice found the flat in St Jerome's square, she thought herself very fortunate. It was situated just behind the old city walls and the sea, and near a motorway to drive to the institute where she was to become a new member of staff. It satisfied her curiosity for historical detail and had a subdued beauty which revealed itself after constant observation. The fountain was its focal point, and the doves with their rhythms gave it a subtle, peaceful harmony. Here I can start afresh, maybe meet some interesting people and have my own space, she thought. She didn't mind how cramped that space was, nor how much she was paying for forty square metres. The peace and quiet, the view of the fountain and the doves from her front and only window were worth it. Barely two months later she was moving out. The hollow feeling inside was threatening to take over her whole being. She didn't quite know when it had started but she had a sneaky suspicion that she wasn't the person she had carefully constructed over the years; in fact, she was struggling not to see a rather useless, well-intentioned and obsessive weirdo who had to have her own way, not so different from the solitary dwellers of the square she was leaving.

The chiming of the church clock tower brings her back to the bare, dusty room and she stifles a pang of regret. She gets up slowly and rings a friend she has made at the institute.

'Hola Juan, I've finished packing. Can you pick me up?'

*✱✱

The 1980s fifth floor apartment Alice now lives in is square, box-like and functional. It is three streets back from the beach which she can see from her balcony. There are no doves, just the occasional squawking sea birds, and in front of her are tall blocks of flats just like hers; the same black iron railings guarding identical balconies in grubby white buildings that are beginning to flake. In the street below, the cars are so tightly parked that you could hardly poke a finger between them. And even with the windows shut there is a constant hum of traffic and occasional irate hooting. Noise invades all. The shouts and screams of young families in her block penetrate the thin walls of Alice's apartment, and she can often hear the conversations and arguments of her next-door neighbours. This new world seems flimsy, weightless, its inhabitants rapidly skimming the surface of their lives like the sea birds skim the sea and then are off swirling high on the next current. The neighbours are curious and gossipy. They want to know where she is from, what she does, does she have a boyfriend? Why is she there on her own? Alice finds herself recoiling from this invasive nosiness. She is the one who now gives a curt 'Bon dia' on the stairs and hurriedly escapes. She goes from room to room in the practical but soulless apartment, wondering where to settle. She has too much space for her few belongings and the overall bareness is felt like an oppressive presence, so much so that she often feels her back is unguarded and must turn quickly to see what or who is there.

Tourists still sunbathe on the long beach and swim in the cooling sea. The warm October sun and softer light attracts many late holidaymakers and third-age Spaniards who walk in throngs along the promenade. Arm in arm they stroll, chattering loudly and looking forward to the next meal in one of the hotels that loom all around the bay. Alice envies their capacity for living in the moment and enjoying small pleasures. They are not wasting their precious time with use-less soul-searching, nor wondering how they made so many mistakes, she thinks. There's the sea, the sun is shining, get out and savour it. But she cannot help being irritated by their hearty cheeriness and by their loud, grating voices. They are an older version of the young hordes that take over the resorts in the summer and convert them into *Bierstrassen*, thus named because of the predominance of German tourists in that area, where alcohol is drunk with straws from plastic buckets and the surviving parts of La Isla de la Calma retreat into dark caves and pray for protection. Fortunately, most of them sleep in a stupor all day on the beach and so leave the rest of the island unscathed. Here money flows in bars and restaurants and endless partying fills the streets every night. There are no homeless, no unpleasant sights to upset the clients, apart from their own vomit.

Alice enjoys the fresh sea air as she takes her strolls along the promenade, imagining there is no concrete, just sand dunes and palms as it was sixty years ago. She can see the gothic cathedral in the distance and below it the ancient walls enclosing the original city. A little way back from the walls lies La Plaça de Sant Jeroni, hidden from view by the façade of St Jerome's church, enshrouded in scaffolding, and the battered stone buildings that face the sea front. On a good day I could walk there in an hour, Alice muses.

She has a few visitors from the institute.

'Nice apartment, Alice, nice apartment. Are you okay here?' are the only comments she receives.

'Yes, I suppose so. It'll take a while to settle in, but at least I have space,' she says dully.

They don't return, and she doesn't really care at all.

***

The school term is well underway, and Alice is in a cocoon of feverish schoolwork. Her pupils are her refuge and she champions them in all their causes. But her colleagues' initial enthusiasm for her pretty face and long legs is waning; she isn't keeping the place allocated to foreign assistants. Which is: entertain the kids but don't bring any of your liberal foreign ideas into the classroom. Alice is no longer an object of desire; she is a threat and must put up with whispered comments in the staff room: 'I wish that bloody woman would stop trying to reform the educational system. Who does she think she is? Little English upstart. We all know nothing works. Have you heard the latest idea she's gone to the Head with? She wants the kids to have the right to assess our teaching and make complaints if they think we're failing or not treating them as well as they'd like. As if we don't have enough trouble already controlling the little buggers.'

'Well, she won't last long here. That type never does,' is the usual end to the conversation.

Alice thinks about applying for teaching posts in institutes on the mainland and abroad, maybe the States? But she is growing tired of wandering, of suspicious blank faces and empty nights.

And now the nightmares. They started a week ago and are punctually insistent. Just before the break of dawn they rise up relentless through the darkness and invade. The whitewashed walls of her apartment are slowly closing in on her until she can hardly turn in her bed. When she is on the point of being bricked in, a reminiscence of medieval torture, she wakes covered in sweat and gasping for breath. No amount of candles, incense and not very successful meditation before bedtime can dispel her anxiety and fear. Sometimes the homeless girl appears just before the walls start falling in on her. The girl has a quizzical expression on her little rat-like face. She is holding an empty bottle of baby cologne and her hair is lank and greasy. 'What do you want?' Alice mouths in her sleep. There is never an answer.

One night the dream is so physically intense that Alice jumps out of bed at five a.m. She knows what she must do. She packs her rucksack with sandwiches and a flask of coffee and sets out. The fresh, silent morning clears her pounding headache as she walks along the sea front towards the city. It is still dark, but she is not afraid. She moves quickly, propelled by a sense of urgency and resolution. Soon the sun begins to rise lazily behind her. It stretches its rosy gold limbs on the sea and slowly illuminates the path before her. She doesn't turn to watch the spectacle but feels the growing light at her back affirming who she is and what she is about to do.

When she is near the square, Alice stops at an all-night chemist. As she comes out the church clock is striking seven. She enters the square and settles down to wait on the damp stone bench. The doves are silent on the dew-drenched seminar rooftop, heads tucked under their wings. A stray dog approaches, sniffs at her ankles and is off searching for scraps. Some lights are on in the flats of her old block, but not in her shuttered window. She tries to suppress the tears that are welling but then gives up and lets them flow freely down her tanned cheeks.

Then an hour later Alice sees the girl shuffle up to the fountain and splash her face with the remaining water in the basin. She is even thinner and her gaunt face has a greyish-yellow tinge; the bloodshot eyes have lost the territorial glint of the wolf. There is no little plastic bag with underwear. She hasn't seen Alice and looks startled when she approaches her.

'Hello, I've got some breakfast and coffee, would you like some?'

The girl, suddenly remembering, gives her a hostile stare.

Alice kneels down and opens her rucksack.

'Look, I've brought this for you.' Alice hands her the bag from the chemist.

The girl hesitates but then snatches the bag and takes out a bottle of baby cologne. She holds it to her for a moment, then, without looking at Alice, slowly applies the cologne to her hair and neck.

'I'll come back tomorrow morning,' Alice says, and leaves the coffee and sandwiches on a bench.

'*Dónde está* Gabriel?' the girl asks. 'I want Gabriel, not you. Why have you come?'

She turns her back on Alice, who looks on speechless and dithering. Then hurried steps ring out on the cobbled stones.

'Elisa don't go!' says a thin young man who looks almost as vulnerable as the girl. He's carrying a flask of coffee and two paper cups. He barely notices Alice in his concern to reach the girl before she leaves the square.

'Sorry, I'm a bit late this morning,' he says and pushes a mass of black hair back from his forehead. 'Come and have some coffee with me.'

Then he notices Alice and the coffee and sandwiches on the bench. 'Oh, I see someone got here before me. Who's your friend?' he asks, looking mildly put out.

'No friend of mine,' says Elisa. 'She can fuck off.' Then, turning to Alice: 'I know who you are. You used to spy on me from that window over there, didn't you? I thought you'd gone. What are you doing here? Come to check up on me, have you? Well, you can sod off now. But thanks for the cologne.' She sneers at Alice with greenish teeth.

Alice and Gabriel smile at each other in recognition. He is the ethereal-looking guy who moved into the apartment above hers.

'Come on, Elisa, don't be like that. Let's all have some coffee together. No one's spying on you. Look, I made this for you.' He pulls out a bracelet made from fine leather strips and set with small turquoise stones.

Elisa takes the bracelet and slips it on her skinny wrist. She gives Gabriel a half-smile.

'Thanks, Gabriel. But I'll have coffee with you tomorrow, just us two, right? I don't want her here,' she says, and leaves the square, cologne in her rucksack and a deadly sway in her step.

'How do you do it?' Alice asks Gabriel.

'Do what?'

'Make friends with her. Gain her confidence. I'm Alice, by the way.'

'Alice. English?' he replies, switching from Spanish to English with a faint Irish accent. 'I don't know. I guess I don't feel pity for her; I just don't want her to feel alone. I want her to think she has a friend who isn't judging her. I never know if she'll come back.'

'So how did you make friends?'

'I painted a picture of the fountain. It was the first thing I painted when I came here. Every day I came down to the fountain in the early morning. The light was perfect then. She would turn up at around eight to have her wash, and she ended up in the painting. She didn't mind. I think it gave her some sense of permanence, of importance even. So I began to share my coffee with her; she's never hungry. We don't talk about her addiction – she's beyond help – or how it began; we talk about anything – the painting, the colour

of the sky, people passing by, some druggie friend of hers —
or nothing at all. I finished the painting, but I still share coffee with her every morning. I only know that she's twenty-
two and she's from Barcelona. She's going downhill fast so
I'm grateful for every day that she turns up, for the hour we
spend together.'

'Can I see the painting sometime?' By now Alice felt she
could ask him anything.

'Sure! Come up now if you like. And you can tell me what
you're doing here! I have to leave at ten to give a class at the
art school.'

That was the first of their meetings in Gabriel's work-
shop apartment; leisurely conversations over coffee and the
contemplation of the paintings that would later be on exhibition in one of Palma's main galleries. Alice loved the
painting of the fountain: the old buildings leaning together
and wreathed in early morning mist; the young girl splashing
her face with water and bathed in the same luminosity as the
fountain. It was as fresh and seductive as Alice's first
glimpse of the square when she had opened the shutters and
wanted to do nothing else but lean on the sill and observe.
The painting was never for sale; it travelled with them over
the years back and forth to England, Ireland, Mallorca.

There was another painting she loved: the final rendering
of the hawthorn tree and the fairy ring at Lough Brin. Gabriel had painted many versions over the years, whenever he
could get back to Ireland. He told Alice its story, about his
Irish ascendency and about Granny Cliona, whose ashes he
scattered around the tree. And through the paintings Alice
fell in love with this man who had left his parent's

comfortable Mallorcan house to be able to paint in the austere little apartment in St Jerome's square.

Gabriel continued to see Elisa every morning, but Alice stayed behind. Once she peeked at them through the half-open shutter but drew back as if she was intruding on a sacred space. One morning in March, Elisa didn't turn up. Gabriel continued to go down every morning for two months with his flask of coffee to wait for her frail figure to come shuffling into the square. She never came back. That summer they also left the square. Alice went back to England, and Gabriel soon followed her.

The Last Months
of
Violet Koski

Seaford, England, 2015–2016

November

I've had a steady drip of visitors. That tells me I'm on the way out. They're all very kind and solicitous, but none of them are going to get me out of here. They sit and chat and eat their and my cake. They try to cheer me up with their forced chatter. I'm grateful really, because they give me a little respite. But after a while I'm so tired I can hardly make a smile, let alone talk, so I say: 'Isn't it time you were going?' Then there's silence.

Gabriel, dear man, dear friend, took me out in the car today. I wasn't feeling so bad, some flashes coming through the spaces between the holes in the old retina. Not a bad day for gloomy November, even a few breaks in the cloud. Gabriel wheeled me to the car and settled me in so effortlessly I didn't feel like a burden for a while. And I actually spotted a tree. Its skeletal fingers pointing to the sky reminded me of my own emaciated, knobbly ones. They're pointing up to what? Like me, when I point to some blur on the horizon. Like me, a walking skeleton with no adorning flesh, they are just plain bark and bone, not one redeeming leaf. I won't get to see the first buds of spring, but to Christmas I must.

Gabriel parked in our favourite place near the cliff tops. I used to be able to make out the Seven Sisters but have to imagine them now. We watched the sea and talked, as we have so many times over the past eight years. I felt the weight of age and illness lighten, my brain cells reviving with the spark plugs of his company and conversation. This friendship has been an unexpected gift. I can tell him how wretched, upset, let down and desperate I feel. He doesn't judge. He nods and listens, but most of all we laugh. Instant rapport and ironic humour to boot. I can ask for little more. Even Douglas liked him and that's saying something, especially with Gabriel being 'one of those arty types'.

I like him to tell me about his childhood and his grand-mother. She died of heart failure when she was sixty-five. Gabriel managed to take her ashes to Ireland when he was twenty, and he scattered them around the hawthorn tree at Lough Brin just as she would have wanted. He's shown me the photo she kept in her living room; I never tire of hearing the story. I secretly wish I was like her, stubborn but authen-tic and far-seeing, and, above all, driven by the love in her big heart. And wouldn't she be so proud of him; a well-known painter and visiting professor of art at Oxford!

In these eight years I've spent as a widow, Gabriel has shown me, just by being the way he is, that there are other ways to live when you knock down all the useless conven-tions. Which are ways to ward off the wolf we think is waiting for us in the dark. Pity it's too late for me.

He's the only person I've ever talked to sincerely about Tim and told how sorrowful, guilty and offended I feel. Those are three powerful emotions all mixed together. I wonder if he could be dead, or eking out a miserable exist-ence, or living an exotic life in some wonderful country. That last option actually hurts more, because why wouldn't he have contacted me? Gabriel tells me so many people go missing and asks did I ever report his disappearance? The fact is, I didn't. I always thought he'd turn up someday when he was destitute, as he usually did when he ran out of money. Douglas said he was on drugs and after their last row practically kicked him out the house, but I just thought it was another of their fights. Looking back, I suppose I should have stood up for him, but I was too aghast at the idea of him taking cocaine and not a word left my mouth. Then I just pushed the horror to the little compartment in my mind labelled 'unbearable situations, thoughts and feelings' and locked it in with all the others.

But I'm sure he's alive somewhere, still full of his old grudges. I always felt used, and I suppose I quite enjoyed the role of Christian martyr. After all, he was educated at Oxford, though we got no thanks for that. And then the years passed, no dead body was found, and I got on with my life.

After an hour up on the cliffs, exhaustion left me speechless. An anchor of solid iron had me weighted to the seat and I needed my bed. This is happening more and more. Tiredness seeps into me. Like dark rain on a black night, it obliterates every part of me. Then I don't care where I am. I just want that airbed and silence. Is that what death is? Darkness and silence?

December

Alice has hung some Christmas baubles over the pictures and put a mini tree next to the unused television. I appreciate her kindness far more than the decorations, which I can hardly make out anyway. She shows me the presents she's bought for the family and tells me the food is all under control. For a while I get caught up in the joy of giving. I've always loved Christmas. Yes, I know it's become commercial and gaudy, but I still love it. It's a good excuse to give presents to people you love, and up till not long ago I got pretty excited about what I was going to get, too. I must be quite sentimental underneath.

The girls will be here soon. That's keeping me going. I'm vomiting more than I used to. Food gets stuck in my throat and some days my heart feels huge, about to burst from its meagre cage of bone. But I keep popping the pills.

Carol and Annie have arrived. They came in damp and steaming from the cold. I'm so pleased, I get quite tearful. Then the nurse comes in.

'There's to be a Christmas quiz in the lounge at five. Why don't you come along, Violet?'

So the girls wheel me to the communal lounge hung with sparkling decorations. We are given paper hats to wear by festive staff. All the old girls and two old boys are placed in a circle, some in wheelchairs, one woman in a bed. A beaming nurse sits in the middle of the circle. She patiently explains the quiz rules: she asks a question. If you get it right, you are given a Cadbury's Roses chocolate. It begins. Half haven't heard the question, some have nodded off and the rest misunderstood it. There is a chorus of 'Eh, what did you say?' interspersed with the lady in the bed shouting out every five minutes, 'I want the lav!' The nurse takes no notice. Me and another lady are answering all the questions. Our mounds of chocolates are growing, and I can feel the ones who are awake glowering at us. The nurse tries asking each one individually and almost puts the answers in their mouths. I feel elated I'm not like them but frightened I will be; these spectres of human beings with most of their faculties worn away, just because they got old. Then the tea urn and cakes are brought in. Most of them scoff it back; nothing wrong with their stomachs. But I have no appetite. I'm a hungry mind dragging an anorexic body and no food will satiate it. I'm wheeled back, the pile of chocolates in my lap. The girls say, 'You were the cleverest of the lot, Mum.' Little consolation that is, as having most of my marbles means being witness to my rapid disintegration.

There's been a bit of a hoo-ha today. The girls have asked if I can go home for the three days of Christmas and sleep there.

'Most certainly not,' Matron says. 'Have you got an air-bed? No? Well, if you haven't got the right equipment, your mother can't sleep there. She will lose her place if she is away for three days. She has to be back by six o'clock at the latest for her pills.'

So bang goes that. I'll be brought and returned by taxi. I'm a visitor to my own home. But we'll see about that ...

Dressing to go out on Christmas Eve and the taxi ride nearly finish me off, but my tongue is hanging out with longing to get to my armchair. I sink into it with such pleasure that I almost feel content. I'm given a Christmas sherry, just a couple of sips, and for a few hours I forget I don't live here. I chat with the girls and pretend to eat a few morsels. By the afternoon I'm a dead weight again and want my air-bed. I'm ready for the taxi half an hour before it arrives. It'd better not happen tomorrow.

Christmas Day. I try to enthuse about the presents I'm given. I won't be wearing or using them. The lunch didn't taste like mine, but they do their best and my back aches so I can hardly sit at the table for five minutes. And again, I have the longing to be in that wonderful bed where I feel so light.

I wish the boys could have been here. They're all too far away, my beautiful grandsons. I've been a better grand-mother than mother. Because I've watched, I've learnt and I've understood. All those conversations and laughter, the lightness and detachment you don't get with your own kids. I'll miss that. That's the worst part of dying. Or maybe the worst are the regrets. They're always lurking there ready to pounce in sleepless nights.

But I'm holding out, today is the day. I'm snuggled in my armchair at quarter to six. The doorbell rings.

'Mum, it's the taxi. I'll help you on with your coat.'

'I'm not going. Tell him to leave.'

'Mum, you know what the matron said.'

'I don't care what she said.'

They both stand there looking helpless, one with my coat, the other with my bag. Then they come towards me and I grip the sides of the armchair.

'Mum, you can't stay here. You know that. You'll be back tomorrow. There isn't the equipment here.'

'I can sleep in my own bed. I'll die where I want.'

They sit down speechless. The taxi is hooting. My heart is racing.

'I told you I'd never go into a home. You can all go away.'

I need to go to the toilet. I hoist myself out of the chair, waving them away. I take two steps and my legs buckle. They catch me before I fall, and then everything goes dark.

'Where am I?'

But the bed tells me I'm back in the home. There are faces peering at me. Someone is holding my hand. Oh well, nice try, Violet. At least I've been a nuisance.

Christmas is over, and I've been thinking about my funeral. It's all planned: the hymns, poems and music. I want it to be a gift from me. And for once I'll be the centre of attention. Even quiet little mice have big egos, you know. I can imagine them all gathered there. Pity I won't be there to see it; or will I? I wonder what they'll say about me.

January

The New Year is here. All I want to do is sleep, not be sick, and have someone dear by my side but not all the time. My hearing is getting worse. Maybe I've got wax. I can't lose that and my sight. Alice still comes and creams my paper-thin skin.

'The sea is like a millpond today, Violet,' she says cheerily.

And then I'm going back, back to Brighton beach. I'm the girl that never tired of watching the sea, who thought I was so lucky living beside this dispenser of free entertainment and wonder. I think about my mother and Polish ancestors struggling to survive, wandering with their black bundles all the way to England. Mum's often here, waiting at the foot of the bed. But not my father, who wasted away from tuberculosis at thirty-two. What was he like? It's strange, but now I don't miss my dead friends and loved ones so much. I can talk to them as if they were around me, and we remember the past together.

February

There have been new developments. My mind is playing tricks on me. Yesterday I saw Annie sitting beside the bed. I recognised her jeans and the way she bends her head when she's reading. There were two men on either side of her. I don't know who they were. I kept asking Annie for a cup of tea but she took no notice of me. I was getting quite irritated when Carol walked in. 'I'm glad you're here,' I said, 'Annie must be going deaf because she won't get me any tea. Look at her sitting there, engrossed in her book.'

Carol tells me that Annie isn't there. 'If they don't answer you, there's no one here.' I'll take her advice because I've seen those men before and they've never answered when I've spoken to them.

Then Gabriel was here. I can't remember if the girls had left or not. I really think there are moments when I'm hallucinating, because I'm sure he told me he'd seen Tim, in Oxford. He's become friends with a homeless guy (typical of Gabriel) who's told him all about his life. Anyway, this man's story and what I told Gabriel coincide, as do names and places. 'Tim couldn't possibly be a homeless man living on the streets,' I said, but I felt the stone in my heart twist sharply. 'Tell him to come and see me then,' I said and turned to the wall. Gabriel said something about me giving him money, that he would talk to Carol and Annie. Could I have dreamt that? I felt a bit disturbed; not the same as when I see those two men. They make me feel peaceful.

I've had to resort to calling the nurse for the commode but at least I'm not wearing pads. Sometimes I only have tea and water all day. But I'm quite peaceful. I'm often back home sitting in my armchair or wandering about my little haven.

A strange thing happened today. I thought I'd died. I was going down the tunnel, seeing clearly for the first time in years; everything was so effortless and diaphanous. Then I heard Carol and Alice's worried voices calling me from far away. So I came back.

'Are the undertakers here?' I asked, convinced this was the moment.

'No, you're still with us.'

I feel annoyed. 'Just how long does it take to die?' I say. I'm fed up with waiting.

My voice is getting fainter. People can't understand what I'm saying half the time and I feel frustrated. Dying is a lonely process.

March

I'm practically at home all the time now, sorting out my things. Sometimes I'm back at the nursing home, but I'm quite peaceful, ready to go.

Annie came today. She held my hand, her head near, trying to hear me. My voice is like a thin reed. 'I should be having six pills now,' I tell her, pointing to my cupped hand. She says maybe I don't remember, but I know perfectly well. I suspect they've stopped my medication.

This morning I asked for toast and marmalade. I love it. But I can't remember if I ate it. I'm so thirsty I keep asking for sips of water. Gabriel has been here. I can still whisper a few words and smile. But I'm a bit agitated. I'm collecting my things, precious bits and bobs. I'm trying to gather it all up but I'm getting frustrated. Gabriel takes my hand and I stop plucking at the sheets. Suddenly I feel peaceful; all hurry to order my things vanishes into an immense calm.

Annie and Alice are here. They give me sips of tea and I lie there, content, half listening to their conversation. My heartbeat is slow, my breath is rasping. Alice creams me and jokes: 'Where have you put them, Violet, under your arms?' She always makes me smile.

It's beginning to get dark. I'm lying on a black sea with no ripple but my own. The swell and surge are lulling me into the sweetest sleep, and I'm back to midnight bathing eighty years ago. I'm being rocked like a babe on a velvet sea and I am filled with love. My heart is about to explode with the immense love I feel for everyone: for Tim, wherever he is, for Douglas and his petty hatreds, for all the people I've known, irritating or good. Nothing matters but this. I'm no longer afraid. Fear stopped me and Douglas from living, but it's disappeared now death is smiling at me. The liquid darkness is engulfing me; down and down, I'm sinking effortlessly. I'm going home at last.

May Morning

Oxford, 2016

My favourite spot is at the end of the Magdalen Bridge, just near Sainsbury's. I rarely go anywhere else. Here I can lean against the wall in a little nook and be sheltered from the wind that funnels up the High Street in the winter months.

Across the road, Magdalen College School still stands in its privileged grounds. It's sealed off from the High Street with its fairy-tale white bridge, sculpted trees and lawns, a microcosm of divine order, at least from the outside. I can watch the boys cross the road in their formal uniforms, chattering in their posh accents, the next generations of the grandiose elite; but underneath they're just snotty-nosed little devils like any state school kid and up to as many spiteful pranks when they can.

I like to watch the people come and go; most of them are students. Quick, quick, they push and laugh, their only worry how to pass the next exam or how to get off with the most recent of their fancies. They are so rooted in their bodies, the flesh firm and solid and real. Not like me. Bits of me are loosening, detaching and falling away. I wouldn't have thought that when I was like them, strutting around in my fresher gown after some event or exam, white carnation in my buttonhole, parading through the crowds of lesser mortals, freshly shaven, my skin plump and shining from good food. No, I wouldn't have thought then that one day I'd slowly dissolve on the pavement.

The gaps are getting wider, stretching out like the holes in my socks, and the draughts blowing through my mind have obliterated any lingering vanity. Now, as I physically diminish, the trees, the lofty Oxford trees of shimmering foliage, and nesting birds fill my empty spaces with their indifferent beauty. And on a good day I even feel a sweet peacefulness. Just let me be overtaken by the air, the river, the sycamore, and I can forget this ragged little self.

The winter is relentless, though. Then the fierce dark side of nature slaps me hard with icy fingers, and freezing fog seeps into my lungs like grey asbestos. Nothing warms my brittle bones, not even layers of flaking cardboard under my sleeping bag in the entrance to Sainsbury's. The skin on my face is red-brown parchment under a grimy woollen hat, and there is a constant dripping of my nose which I wipe away with the back of my hand. There must be a permanent black streak across my cheek. If I'm lucky enough to have made five quid, I can get into a shelter for the night and have a bowl of soup. But sometimes I'm too tired to walk there. So I curl into a ball and wish I still had my dog, Chia, to warm me. She was as scabby as me in the end and only survived a couple of winters. I don't want to make another one suffer what I do. And now there's some plan afoot to fine us for sleeping rough; an ironical 2,500 quid!

But it's April, there's still hope. That's if I can survive the onslaught of memories it always brings. As T. S. Eliot's poem goes: 'April is the cruellest month.' He knew. As the sap rises it stirs everything, good and bad, sweet and bitter. Most of my padding has worn away and the sap stings my thin veins. Life awakening hurts like putting numb fingers into a bowl of warm water.

April nights are softer and more promising. My ear has become attuned to the heavy silence of the dark and to the sound of the murky river flowing under the bridge. I'm a bit bent, but when I can unfurl myself, I cross the road and walk up to the centre of the bridge and look over the side where the school is. I like doing that in the early spring morning when no one is around and I won't horrify the tourists. It's not often I can have a wash, only when I get into the shelter. But at that hour I can watch the morning mist rise from the river and gently enshroud the lawns and buildings. No one exists but me and the creaking boats whispering to each other in the uncanny dawn. The eternal gift of dawn. Then the birds, those callers to prayer, start their chorus, and for five minutes I am in an earthly paradise.

April is the prelude to the one event in the year that keeps me alive: May Morning. On the first of May at 6 a.m. the Magdalen College Choir sings from the top of the college bell tower. They begin with the 'Hymnus Eucharisticus' and continue with madrigals that honour and welcome the merry month of May. The crowds gather along the High Street and the bridge, and I am part of that crowd. There are always students in formal clothes, the overspill from all-night balls. But however drunk they are, no one perturbs the silence as the choir assembles at the top of the tower. The wing of an angel lightly brushes us all.

When the choir sings, we are one harmonious body, pacified by those exquisite voices. Then there are no differences of class, colour and smell. And for a short moment in time reality intensifies. The scale of colours and sound is magnified and our feeble senses become sensitive enough to discover them. It's like being on an LSD trip without the crashing aftermath.

You will be wondering how I know the name of the first hymn in Latin, and why I like to be near the Magdalen College School. Or maybe you have already guessed that I was a chorister; that I was one of those boys chosen for the purity of their voices; that I was one of the elite; that I was there in the front pew of the gothic chapel, brown-eyed and brown-haired, singing to heaven with the ease of a nightingale; that I helped to create the sound that made even the most doubtful believe in the sacred for forty minutes.

When I look at the white wooden bridge I crossed so many times, I remember my childhood there, as unreal and swift as fleeting images on a screen. Did I play in those grounds, fresh and rosy-cheeked? Did I rehearse for hours with the choirmaster, cross the road every day in my miniature academic gown and enter the dark splendour of the Magdalen chapel, laden with solemnity, the works of art hanging heavily in the shadows, the damp air pushed upwards by the purity of our voices?

The schedule was hard: at 7.30 a.m. practice before school and immediately afterwards; choral evensong six nights a week in term, and on Sundays, rehearsal at 9.30 a.m. before the Eucharist. Then afternoon practice followed by evensong at 7 p.m. We were trained like professionals. The master used to say that this training would stay with us for the rest of our lives. He was right. It does. The music is encrusted in my brain and heart. I can remember the hymns, some in Latin, German, French, even Russian. We learnt piano, went on tours, sang in concerts and travelled abroad. From the age of seven this was my life.

My parents didn't take much interest; they were just pleased that as a chorister two-thirds of the school's tuition fees were paid by the college. And they had me out of their way. They were always conspicuously missing from the parents' social group and the services. It was like being at boarding school except that I slept and ate dinner at home. The choir was my surrogate family, not the highly disciplined team it was for the other boys.

I was the eldest and weirdest of their three children, and my father chose me to discharge his violent temper and frustrations on; just my presence was enough to get the drums rolling, and the underside of my bed became the best shelter from his molten rage. To this day I don't understand what it was in me that sparked that hatred, and sometimes in my darkest moments the terrified child still emerges. And what better place to hide than the streets of Oxford, where I've become a voyeur of other people's lives?

And my mother. All she wanted was a quiet life, no confrontation and time away from him and his temper. She concentrated on my younger sisters, who didn't 'get above themselves' singing in elite choirs. She was sceptical of all organised religion and never set foot inside a church 'where all those hypocritical buggers gather and then go home and kick the cat.' Somewhere along the years we lost each other, but first she lost herself, being married to him. She was of Polish, Jewish origin and my father never let her forget her humble beginnings, that he had 'saved her from poverty and given her a comfortable life.'

My voice broke at thirteen, but I continued as a choral scholar right up to my undergraduate years. The choir upheld me. I learnt to become still, to listen, to fall into the depths of sound. When I sang, I stepped into a parallel world of beauty and love where there were no beatings, no hiding under the bed, no desperate loneliness.

So I am waiting for the May Morning chorus to anoint us one more year. In the meantime, I sit in my corner and wish I could catch a glimpse of the College meadows, filled with green-purple flowers at this time of year, or watch the wandering deer feeding on the lush pastures. Instead, I watch people, especially the girls who wear their beauty like plates of armour, smooth and shiny and bold: 'Look at me, no, not you. You are unworthy to look at me in my splendour.' But as they get older the metal gets tarnished, a little thin in places until a few hairline cracks appear. One day it disintegrates on the field of battle and their poor naked souls quiver. Then they beg for a glance, just like their less beautiful sisters always have done. And even a smile from a homeless guy contents them.

I'm quite well known by the locals. Some give me bits of food, the odd quid, bottles of water. Other passers-by, those supercilious ones, avert their eyes or tut-tut: 'When is the council going to do something about this?' They think I'm on drugs or an alcoholic, but I'm stoned on life, not on the aids to make it bearable.

But there is one guy who always stops to talk to me. Twice a week he gives me five quid so I can go to the shelter. He's tall, thin, with greying black hair, probably in his fifties. At first I thought he was a social worker, except that he isn't like the other ones who are always trying to get you into an institution. No; he's different. He's different because he listens and seems to understand. When we talk it's like we were sitting on a sofa drinking tea and eating chocolate biscuits. It's easy. He sees me, not a grubby homeless guy. Bit by bit I've told him my life story, although sometimes we just joke and talk about the weather. When he's gone, I feel as light as air. He's the only one who knows how I ended up on the streets of Oxford; he's the only one worthy of knowing my story. He doesn't judge; he cares from the soul.

And how did a little rich boy end up homeless in the glorious city of Oxford? I told him – Gabriel – how I got a degree in philosophy at Magdalen College. It was so hard that the cocaine circled among many of us to get through the exams. In my second year I was a Zen Buddhist and would wander about the streets in a black tunic like some kind of monk waiting for enlightenment. I tried to eliminate the need for all sensory forms, including art, so there were no barriers, not even beautiful ones, between me and the sublime. But I couldn't do without music. By then I was not a welcome figure in the choir and was asked to leave. In the third year the cocaine had me on the verge of madness, my father luckily disowned me and I just managed to pass my finals.

And what do you do with a third-class degree in philosophy? I went from one soul-destroying job to another, got kicked out of them all for my insolence, until I had no money for rent and no girl would put up with me. Contact with my parents finished at the age of twenty-two; what was the point? When I left home, my father could no longer feed on my fear and died of heart failure at fifty-four. So the street gradually became my home, which suited me as a lonely wanderer. I didn't fit anywhere, nor do I want to now.

There isn't much time left. All that remains is some fleeting beauty I can grasp at and the memory of the choir.

And what happened to my mother? A couple of months ago Gabriel came with some story about this old woman in a nursing home who his wife looks after, down in Seaford. He said she was called Violet Koski, which was my mother's maiden name, and that she could possibly be my mother as all the details fit. Would I like to go and see her, just to make sure? She didn't have much longer to live, he said. He would drive me down and take care of everything. I looked at him agape. 'Gabriel,' I said, 'can't you see it's too late? Even if she is my mother, the thread was broken years ago. You are more real to me than her. What could I say to her? What could she say to me? She'd probably die of fright anyway. Better to leave things as they are. Thanks anyway, mate. You're the nearest thing to love and affection I've felt in my life.'

In March, Gabriel came back from a visit to Seaford. He told me Violet had passed away on the tenth. He pressed a photo into my hand. It was one of me and my sisters with my mother on Brighton beach. I was about ten and we all looked pinched with cold and miserable. 'Promise me you won't tear it up,' Gabriel said. I can't deny him anything, so I slipped it into my pocket and said nothing.

I was telling myself my story, as I often do, colouring it with new details and most likely muttering, when Gabriel came to see me. He was flustered, in a hurry, unusual for him. He placed five quid in my hand and said:

'Listen, Tim, I want you to go to the shelter tonight and have a shower. I'm coming back tomorrow same time. Make sure you're clean, eh? I have something for you.'

And he was off, rushing along the bridge, long hair whipped off his brow. I wonder what's got into him. I can't be that smelly; I had the last shower at least a week ago. I missed our chat, but we'll have one tomorrow.

Now it's the next day. I've had my shower and am waiting. I hope he's not going to give me a goodbye present, but my intuition is telling me he is. He rarely talks about himself, so I don't know much about his life. I'm a self-centred old sod.

Here he is, out of breath and red-faced. He's carrying a large plastic bag. He sits down beside me on the ground and opens the bag. He takes out a beautifully tailored black coat, a Burberry.

'Come on, mate. Get up. I want you to put this on, see how it fits,' he says, and helps me up.

Agape, I shed my ancient duffle coat and pull on the silk-lined Burberry. It fits perfectly.

'I can't wear this. It looks ridiculous on me, much too expensive for a homeless old codger. I'll be a laughingstock.'

'I got it from a charity shop, a bargain! And you're wearing it anyway, so no protesting. You'll need it where we're going. Afterwards you can put on your old coat again if you feel more comfortable, but it's yours to keep,' he says, and gives me a playful shove.

'Where the hell are you taking me?' I'm getting agitated. 'Can't we just have a chat? Look, I've got some chocolate biscuits!'

'You'll see. You need some exercise, always sitting on your lazy arse in this corner. Come on!'

It's Gabriel, so I trust him. No one else would I allow to take my arm and propel me gently over the bridge. We walk at my pace, although I know he'd be running. I can sense the nervous excitement under his silence. When we get to Magdalen College entrance he stops and says:

'It's quarter to six. We're just in time for evensong.'

Before I can open my mouth, he pulls me through to the porter's lodge and says to the two burly guys behind the thick glass screen:

'We're going to the chapel for evensong. Did you know this gentleman used to be a chorister here?'

They look at me, aghast. No Burberry coat can transform my face and hair, but they wave us on. I am trembling with anticipation and shock. Gabriel puts his arm around my shoulder and we walk the well-known path to the chapel. People are waiting in line outside in the dark corridor, but the guy at the chapel door seems to know Gabriel and we are ushered in first. How has he managed that? I'm beginning to suspect that he's a respected figure in Oxford, maybe even someone important.

It's as I remember. The dark wood glistens, the white-grey walls and pillars are just as sombre in their cold magnificence. The candles in the glass holders flicker and beckon along the wooden stalls. 'Come and sit,' they seem to say. 'This is reality; the chaos outside is just a bad dream.'

I shuffle behind Gabriel, who finds the best seats, the best angle to watch and listen. I sit next to him, my head down, my nose dripping. I'm glad I had a shower.

'Tim, you can come here when you want. Just put on your Burberry coat and the guy at the door will let you in, even if I'm not with you,' he says, but he doesn't look me in the eye.

I am speechless. Gabriel gives me a handkerchief to stop me wiping the tears and snot away with the back of my hand. I'd forgotten what it's like to cry. But I must lift my matted head; I must watch. The stalls are filling. The wood creaks under the slow-moving feet. People stare at me and then politely turn their well-groomed heads. I sit closer to Gabriel and look down again. I shouldn't be here; the grotesque ghost of a former chorister can only linger in gloomy corners. I'm thinking of slinking out when the bell rings.

The choir enters, master at the fore. They are wearing the same red cassocks and white surplices. Sixteen young boys, well-scrubbed fake angels, take their places meekly. The twelve choral scholars, bursting with youth and well-directed testosterone, sit further up behind them and survey the audience with a subtle air of superiority. Nothing has changed.

The service begins. The choir sing the first hymn. I lean forward, away from Gabriel's protective bulk. I hear a thud and Gabriel picks up the book of psalms I've knocked onto the floor. I have forgotten who I am, my aching bones and my empty stomach. I have soared to the vault on the sound wave of those voices. I am singing with them; I am there in the front row in my usual place, the purest, highest notes flowing easily from my young throat. All my broken parts are sealed together, like those Japanese vases whose cracks are filled with gold. I am the child, the youth, the philosophy graduate, the homeless beggar; no piece is missing, nothing is lost. This is my place. At least, for forty minutes, this is home.

When it's over and the procession, ethereal in the candlelight, has left the chapel, Gabriel and I wait till everyone has left. I am trembling and must hold onto his arm. He invites me to coffee and cake in a High Street café. But I refuse. You can fill a patched-up vessel once; twice is asking for trouble.

'Come on, mate, you're wearing your new coat! What's up?' he says, but I know he understands.

The truth is that I need to get back to my place by Sainsbury's. I need to feel the pavement under me and the roughness of my old coat. I want the night to come and the stillness before dawn; I want my emptiness and the peace it brings. I wouldn't mind if I died tomorrow. I would float off with the music of the choir resounding in my head, but, above all, I would be buoyed up on my journey by the love of this man, Gabriel.

Acknowledgements

I wish to thank Nicky Taylor for her sensitive and expert editing.

I am eternally grateful to Marie Timlin for showing me the photo of the fairy ring near Lough Brin which inspired Gabriel's story. She was also my inspiration for the character of Cliona.

My thanks also to Alicia Miñano who lived in the square around the fountain and whose description of the drug addict who washed there gave me the idea for the story of The Fountain.

My thanks to friends and family who read the manuscript and gave me invaluable feedback: my sister Linda, my sons Steven and David, the late, beloved Patricia German and her daughters Sian and Glynis, Irene, Xisco Maturana, Jon Bowra, Marie Timlin and her daughters Cathy, Tonia and Cristina and Brendan Timlin.

I am very grateful to the following people who took the time and trouble to read the manuscript and write blurbs:

Alice LaPlante, Cecilie Gamst Berg, Elaine Kingett and Barbara Jago.

About the Author

Heather Smith was born in Brighton, England in 1950. She studied English and Philosophy at Manchester University for two years before, aged twenty, she made the move to Mallorca, Spain.

A degree in Spanish Philology from the University of the Balearic Islands (UIB) followed and, in 2017, she was awarded an MA in Creative Writing from Oxford Brookes University.

Since retiring from teaching A-level English at a Majorcan secondary school, she dedicates her time to translation projects, running a book club and her own writing which she does in both English and Spanish.

In 2018 she published a book of poems: *Poems of Joy and Melancholy* (Ars Poetica, Oviedo, Spain). She contributed to a book of stories about Oxford in Spanish: *Relatos de El Trueno Dorado* (Editorial Sapere Aude). Having recently finished a fictionalised memoir, she is currently writing short stories.

Heather is a widow and has two sons and four grandchildren.

www.ingramcontent.com/pod-product-compliance
Lightning Source LLC
Chambersburg PA
CBHW061459210726
48287CB00007B/2583